Salem Charm

Salem Charm

Book 3 of Colson Brothers Series

REESE MADISON AND LYNNE FOSTER

authorHOUSE®

AuthorHouse™
1663 Liberty Drive
Bloomington, IN 47403
www.authorhouse.com
Phone: 1-800-839-8640

Published by AuthorHouse   04/01/2013

ISBN: 978-1-4817-3704-3 (sc)
ISBN: 978-1-4817-3703-6 (e)

Library of Congress Control Number: 2013906031

We would like to dedicate this love story to Mr. & Mrs. Louis and Barbara Early. Your love kept us close as a family, and inspired those who knew you to accept nothing less than a true and everlasting love. We miss you more than words can ever express. Lou and Barbara are native North Carolinians who retired in Oriental, NC where their son still resides.

Prologue

"Are you kidding me? North Carolina? I just got back here!" I complained when Slider gave me the order. 'Here' being the Arizona desert. Forty miles east of Phoenix in a small town called Apache Junction to be exact.

"Sorry Bro, but it's important we get the bitch out of there. Mr. Whitmore, her father, is paying us a hundred thousand dollars to ensure her safety. Some kind of deal went bad sending him into hiding. Now he wants us to get her as far away from the situation as possible."

"I know I can protect her, it's what I do. What I *don't* like is going back into Chardonnay's territory. If she finds out one of her half brothers is in the house, It's going to stir up a shit storm." I told him what he already knows, all too well. She's his full-blood younger sister, and Turner's twin sister. Turner is one of the, scratch that, he is the meanest, and probably the biggest, of all us brothers.

"Yeah, I wouldn't wear your cut once you cross the Mississippi. Do you have an old leather without a patch?"

"Fuck no." Of course I don't. I've been a member since I was eighteen, almost ten years now. I don't own another jacket. On the rare occasions I do go back east, I go quickly, and put a plain grey sweatshirt I own over my leather to cover my patch. We're allowed to do that when the job is considered 'under cover', especially outside our territory.

"Go buy one." Slider waved me off after handing me an envelope. "And hurry up. I want this shit over with."

"Yeah yeah." I went through the bar and outside to the parking lot where my large, overpacked, Electra Glide waited for me in all her glory. All she needs is long-legged woman to grace the seat behind me, and I could die a happy man.

It's been so long since I've gotten laid my nuts are turning blue. There's been no time. I'm a Transporter. I get paid insane amounts of money to get people into hiding. Normally I keep my work on the west side of the Mississippi, but the club could use this chunk of change. The club always needs money. Charities will suck your wallet dry if you let them. Slider's wife loves charities.

One of Stacy's girls, Ginger I think is her name, came sauntering over in high heels too tall for such short legs while I geared up for the long ride across country. "Leaving us already Lou?"

"Yes dear, a man has to work for a living you know." I informed her sarcastically.

"You don't have to tell me." She batted her over made up eyelashes at me. "How about a hand job before you go? I'll give you a special discount . . ." She asked with an exaggerated, ridiculously fake, flirt.

Ah hell. I've been avoiding her all week. I don't do whores because there's something fundamentally wrong about paying for sex. At least to me there is. When I'm with a woman I need her to want to be there for me, and not the money.

But a hand job? Well, I guess I can do that. It *has* been a while. "Make it quick." I reached for my wallet and let her pick out the the price of her service.

She tucked the twenty into her bra and pulled my zipper down. The hand job turned into a forty dollar blow job. Oh well, it was worth it. She turned out to be a lot better with her mouth than just her hand. That and there was something erotic about fucking her mouth right there in the parking lot.

The relief of not being sexually pent up set the right tone for the ride across country. I rode hard and fast making the journey in thirty-eight hours or so. I didn't exactly watch the clock along the way. I rode until I had to sleep and eat, then kept going.

I met my contact, Myles, at a run down gas station just outside of Raleigh, North Carolina. He's about ten years older than me and looks like a retired Marine. According to my information he's been the girl's body guard most of her life. I wonder if he's a wannabe Marine, or if he actually served.

We shook hands, caught each other up on the case, then I followed him to the plantation where I'm to pick up the girl. Barbara Whitmore. Even the name sounds stuck up.

When I saw the house, excuse me, mansion, I knew I was in for a long ride back with this woman. I bet she's dumb as an ox and wearing some fancy dress with stupid flowers all over it. She probably squeaks when she walks.

Myles handed me the keys to the Mercedes CLS63 AMG he'd been driving. "I'll send your bike back on the rails. Slider said he will have it picked it up for you."

I took the keys and off-loaded my bags to the back seat of the car that costs about as much as I make in half a year. "Thanks. I'll have to ditch the car along the way. I'll let you know where to pick it up."

"No problem, we have about eight of the damn things." He complained.

"In other words it won't be missed." I laughed. Rich people. Imagine, a million dollars in disposable cars. What a waste.

"Not for a while. Mr. Whitmore has always been wealthy, and very protective of Miss Barbara. A couple cars is a small price to pay to keep her safe as far as he's concerned." He handed me an envelope. "Mr. Whitmore told me to give you this. I'm sure it's traveling money."

I tucked the envelope in my inside jacket pocket. The jacket I begrudgingly picked up at a dealer in Albuquerque. "Not necessary, but I'll take it." The real money would have been wired directly to Slider. He'll take his cut and hand me mine when I get back that way.

Myles laughed, "Come on in so we can retrieve Miss Whitmore. I should warn you, she's a feisty one."

"Feisty?" She probably has long lacquered fingernails.

"She has no idea what's going on. As far as she knows her father is still in New York with his latest conquest. She's not going to want to leave, and if she does, she'll want to go wherever he is. She tends to think she can fix everything."

"Great."

1

"I beg your pardon??" I stood as Myles finished explaining the presence of who I now know as Mr. Louis Colson. Or Lou, as he has informed me he would prefer to be addressed.

"I'm sorry Miss Barbara, but I have strict orders from your father." Myles apologized.

Lou looked at Myles, "Do you work for her, or her father?" He asked sharply.

My body guard, and lifelong friend, shot him a dirty look before replying, "Her father."

"Well then, let's get on with it." Lou stepped around the left side of my desk looking like he was coming for me.

I stepped to the right side trying to escape and put my hand up palm out, "Now look sir, I have no intention of going anywhere with you. If I need protecting I have a perfectly good body guard right here." I looked at Myles.

Myles shook his head. "Not this time. Lou is the best Miss Barbara, please let him do his job. Your father hired him specifically because he is the best. You know how he is about your safety and well-being." Myles reminded me.

"No!! I do not feel safe with this . . ." I looked at Lou again. He's tall, slender with broad shoulders, and in desperate need of a haircut. "biker." It was obvious Lou had been riding. Motorcycle gear isn't all that different than horseback riding gear. His leather is black, where as mine is brown.

Next thing I know Lou lunged, grabbed me around the middle with long fingers, and hoisted me over his shoulder with my rump in the air. "Sorry Barbie, but I have a job to do." He doesn't sound sorry one bit.

"Put me down right now minute!!" I can't believe I'm resorting to yelling. Ladies don't yell. The Salem Academy For Girls saw that each student conducted herself as a proper lady. I was no different.

He carried me through the house, out the front door, and deposited me harshly in the passenger seat of a familiar Mercedes. He reached across my middle and buckled my belt. His unshaven face is an inch from mine. "Stay." He ordered.

"I will not." I informed him as I tried to unfasten the seatbelt.

He took my hands and produced handcuffs from somewhere behind him and slapped them over both of my wrists. "You won't get far in those heels and your hands bound, so don't try it." He ducked back out and shut the door hard in my face. How rude!! I don't care how crystal bright blue those eyes are. I've never seen eyes so blue. Stop thinking about his eyes Barbara. Did he call me Barbie a few minutes ago.

My blood boiled hotter as I watched him exchange a few words with Myles before he came around to get in the driver's seat. He barely glanced at me before throwing the car in gear and sending gravel flying everywhere.

"Would you kindly slow down? The drive was just raked two weeks ago."

"No." He replied and turned up the radio.

"I'm talking to you, please turn that down." I fished around for a bobby pin that's holding my hair in a french twist.

"There's nothing to talk about." He informed me dryly.

"I believe there is. What is going on with my father?" I found the pin I wanted and pulled it free. My hair stayed up nicely, good. I have a new hair spray my girlfriend recommended. At the time I wasn't sure it would hold as well as my old one, which has recently been discontinued much to my dismay.

He sighed, "All I know is he's in trouble, which means you're in trouble. Now he's paying me a shit load of money to get you as far away from his mess as possible. Whatever else I may know, or not know, is of none of your concern. Just sit there and be quiet, it's going to be a long fucking drive across country."

"Watch your language Mr. Colson, you are in the presence of a lady." I scolded him as the first lock popped releasing my left cuff.

He looked down at the sound, "What the . . . did you just use a hairpin to unlock that?" His surprise is my own little victory.

"Yes, it's not rocket science, it's a simple lock." I started work on the other one, but it's a little more difficult left-handed. Myles taught me this trick when I was ten and home sick with a cold bug. I was bored and cranky. I guess he thought it was better than watching the idiot box. I agree, especially today.

"I have cable ties, so watch it." He warned me.

"I have no intention of being bound again. I need my purse, go back."

"No. No purse, no going back. We're going east first to throw off anyone who might have been watching that ridiculously large plantation, then we'll double back west. My brother will pick us up for a bit, after he see's us to Phoenix I'll get my bike and we'll go where I know I can keep you safe. Aside from that, there is no other information I can give you." He looked over at me. His eyes went down, then back up.

"Do not look at me like a piece of meat Mr. Colson."

"I'm wondering how you can move in that stiff ass suit." He shook his head when he put his eyes back on the road.

"I move just fine." I assured him as I pulled on the hem of my skirt down as far as I could towards my knees.

The wiggle and shift in my seat was un-lady like to say the least. I hope this nonsense is over with soon. I have work to do! Boring work, but it still needs to be done. I need to call and make sure everyone knows what's going on. Myles will fill them in I'm sure.

"I bet you do." He replied enjoying his joke.

"Pardon me?" My mind had wandered so I was no longer sure what he was talking about.

"Nothing. Are we done talking yet?" He's annoyed again. So much for his sense of humor.

"Yes. I am quite through conversing with you."

"Good." He reached for the knob again and turned it to a country music station. Not a very good one, but country is more civilized than most, so it will do.

For about the next three hours we took back roads east towards the ocean. I don't get out very often to explore my home state of North Carolina, so I'm trying to distract myself by enjoying the scenery. So far I've seen rundown house after another, and one large pine tree after another. Not enough stimulation to keep me from obsessing in my head about what kind of mess my father has gotten himself into.

Myles had refused to tell me anything other than I was in danger and to go with Lou. I wish I'd grabbed my purse. At least then I could call my father.

When I saw the sign for Oriental in five miles I reached up to turn the radio down. "Are we going to this Oriental?" I asked because there doesn't seem to be anything but water coming our way on the GPS.

"Yes. I have contacts there. You need to change your look." He glanced over and gave me that up and down thing again.

"Stop looking at me like that. And pray tell, what is wrong with my attire?" I crossed my arms in a huff.

"Your *attire*, Miss Whitmore, screams rich spoiled southern belle, which is exactly what they'll be looking for. We'll stay here for a night, then we'll double back west to meet my brother Turner and his old lady tomorrow afternoon."

"With whom are we meeting?"

"Turner, one of my brothers. He has a tight RV he and my other brother Joe have been working on for years. I've heard Joe talk about it, and Turner finally came out of hiding to get married, so I'm calling in a favor. For the money your father is paying the club I can spare a few bucks to do this right. If anyone gets past Turner it'll be a first." He assured me.

"I don't have money for new clothing."

He reached into his inside jacket pocket and tossed an envelope in my lap. "I'm sure you can find something with this. Keep it simple. Jeans, t-shirt, tennis shoes. And take your hair out of that ridiculously stiff knot. Put it in a ponytail if you must, but that hairdo screams tight rich bitch."

"Mr. Colson! I will remind you to watch your language." I opened the envelope. There's about fifty grand in here. Good. Maybe I can buy my way out of this rude man's rude care.

He snatched the envelope back. "I'll be keeping that after all."

"That's my father's money, in effect, *my* money. Give it back." I held my hand out palm up.

"No ma'am. I saw that look on your face. Keep it up and I'll put you in the trunk." He threatened.

"You will do no such thing."

"Watch me." He slowed as we came into town. "This is a small town. Everybody knows everybody, and everybody knows me. If you try to run it's going to not only embarrass you, but will most likely piss me off. Pissing off the man being paid so much money to protect you is not smart Miss Whitmore. Try to remember that."

I pouted hating that I'm in this situation, and in this car with this biker. He's crude, rude, and I hate his voice. He's so condescending.

Lou took a left just before a bridge threatened to take up to what is no doubt a swamp of an island. A long block later he took a right and parked in front of a very rundown antique store. He got out and came around to open my door. "Let's go Miss Whitmore. Nobody will look twice at you in secondhand clothes."

"What exactly do you expect me to find in there?" I asked stepping out of the car because I want to stretch, not appease him.

He shut the door behind me, grabbed my arm and got in my face. His light blue eyes are *not* happy as they dance over mine. "You're going to wear exactly what I tell you. I'm being paid to keep you safe, not happy. You'd be well served to remember that. The trunk is always an option."

"You have horrid breath, and you need to learn what a razor is used for." I replied.

His eyebrows came together in the middle a little, "I haven't had a shower in two days because I've been hauling ass across the country to save your pretty little ass, and I have no intention of shaving." He stood upright to his full height, which is quite a bit more than I originally thought.

"I suggest you buy a toothbrush while we're in here." I instructed. Did he just say I was pretty? When was the last time someone said anything nice about me? Certainly never *to* me.

"I have a toothbrush Miss Whitmore, just not the opportunity to use it recently." He held the door for me and shoved me inside with his meathook of a hand gripping my arm.

I looked around and had to put my hand over my nose and mouth. This place reeks of mold and dust.

"Aww, is the little southern belle appalled?" He teased pulling me towards the back. "You have exactly fifteen minutes to pick out a few days worth of clothes. We need to hurry up and get food and sleep if we're going to meet Turner and his new bitch on time tomorrow."

"Language Mr. Colson. Women are not 'bitches'." I schooled him.

"They are to me, especially the one talking back to me right now." He snapped at me.

"Excuse me Mr. Colson! You will not speak to me in such a manner!"

He leaned down into my ear, "I will speak to you any way I please. Now get dressed before I do it for you."

I smacked him hard across the face before quickly retreating to the other side of the clothing rack.

He looked at me and smiled as he ran his hand over his whisker clad jaw, "Foreplay will get you everywhere Miss Whitmore."

"That, was *not* foreplay." I assured him.

"You wouldn't know foreplay if it hit *you* in the face." He argued.

"Oh!! You are an insufferable, rude, smelly, beast of a man."

"Why thank you. That's the nicest thing you've said all day." He teased and stood back folding his arms to watch as I sifted through the clothes.

I wound up finding an ill fitting pair of jeans, boots that were surprisingly comfortable, and a few shirts that would do. I also found a well worn leather jacket in a dark camel color I that is right nice.

We paid for our purchases after I changed clothes in the back room, then he took me to some hole in the wall restaurant next door. It's really more of a bar than a restaurant. The food was greasy and the music way too loud, yet somehow it was comfortable.

After supper he drove us to what I thought would be an appropriate hotel overlooking the water from across the street. I found myself looking forward to the view from my room as he parked, and some privacy. Surely he's planning on getting two rooms.

Wrong. He not only ordered one room, he then proceeded to specifically request one bed. I tried to protest, but he clamped his hand over my mouth. The lady handed him the key with a smile. She must be one of his many contacts in this odd little town.

Once inside the room he all but pushed me into the bathroom. "I've had about enough of you. Use the restroom if you need it, then I'm going to take a shower and get some sleep."

I slammed the door in his face and turned to look in the mirror. "Oh good Lord." I look like I've been wind-blown. My hair is a fright, these clothes are just plain filthy under all this light. Oh how I could use a long hot bath and a SoCo on the rocks.

I took my time freshening up before finding him standing just outside the door. "It's all yours."

"I'm going to take a shower. Don't go anywhere or you'll sleep in the trunk."

"May I use your phone to call Myles?"

"No." He picked it up off the dresser and pointed at me, "Are you going to behave?"

"Tell me why I can't call my bodyguard."

"Because he doesn't know where you are, and that's how it's going to stay until I say otherwise."

"How do I know I can trust you?"

"Are you still alive?"

"Obviously Mr. Colson."

"Then you can trust me. Lay down and get some sleep, tomorrow is going to be a long day." He disappeared into the bathroom, then stuck his head back out to add, "Don't use the land line either. I have my reasons for not giving up our location just yet."

"Go take your shower Mr. Colson, we can discuss this when you no longer smell like a pig."

He shut the door firmly before letting loose a string of cuss words pertaining to me that I'm sure I've never heard in such fluid force. The devil on my shoulder giggled.

Lou finished his shower a little while later so I closed my eyes and pretended to be asleep. I can hear him moving about. The fresh scent of lemon and soap tickling my nose now was oddly soothing.

"You can open your eyes now Barbie." He informed me finally.

I did and immediately closed them again. "Please put on your pants."

"I'm don't wear my jeans to bed, unless I have to, and here in a hotel room, I don't have to." He crawled onto the bed and brought his long arm around my middle to pull me against him so my back is to his chest.

"Get some sleep, tomorrow is going to be a long day." He wrapped his hand around my wrists.

"Get your hands off me."

"No. I need to make sure you can't get away."

"I can't move Mr. Colson."

"Precisely why you'll stay right where you are, now hush."

"How am I supposed to sleep with your big mitts all over me?"

"Honey, if my 'big mitts' *were* all over you, sleeping would be the last thing on your mind."

I tried to kick him but he put his big heavy leg over both of mine pinning me firmly in place. "Oh boy, more foreplay."

"You're going to pay for this Mr. Colson." I promised as I talked myself out of biting him.

"If it involves your lips and your hips, I'll suffer. Now hush, I have duct tape." He threatened.

"You wouldn't dare."

"Yes, I would dare, now, be quiet."

"I hate you."

He shook with a short laugh from behind me, "You smell like me."

"Not by choice."

"You make a good pillow too." He nuzzled his face into my hair and neck.

"Stop that."

"You're fluffy."

I couldn't stop the laugh that escaped, "Fluffy?? Are you serious?"

He moaned and hugged me to him. "Fluffy and soft, when you're not all tied up in tight suits and pantyhose."

"Go to sleep before I change my mind about running away to call Myles and tell him what an awful man you are."

"Awful. Terrible. Beastly." He inhaled deeply, "What is that, lotion?"

"Goodnight Mr. Colson."

I must have fallen into a deeper sleep than I expected because next thing I know someone is rolling me over and there's a heavy warm weight covering me.

"Mmmm. You still smell good." Lou's voice brought me back to reality quickly.

"Get off me!!!" I pushed hard against his chest.

He lifted up in a push-up over me with a smile that is annoying to say the least. "Sleep good?"

"No!" I kicked but it had little effect the way his legs are trapping mine.

He lowered his head and whispered in my ear. "I am not a sick pervert. You are perfectly safe with me. But you do smell damn good." He hopped off taking my hand along the way pulling me along with him for me to stand up. "Go get ready. We leave in an hour." He smacked me on the rear end.

"Ow!!" I spun around and smacked him across the face again. "That hurt!!"

He stalked me to the bathroom with a playful yet hunting look in his eyes.

I walked backwards with my finger pointed at his nose, "Stay away from me."

"Go. Get. Ready." He insisted slowly.

"I would if you didn't look like you were going to pounce on me."

He smiled a wicked smile, "Trust me, it's a thought. Go." He pointed to the door. "Now. By the way, you look much prettier without all the make-up."

I turned and grabbed the door to shut in his face. Geez that man is a conundrum. One minute he's telling me I smell good. The next he's smacking me on my rump, then a minute later he's flirting with me?? And why is he so mean at times?

"Where is my car??" I looked around for the beautiful piece of machinery. I think we were in the Mercedes Myles usually drives. He's going to miss that car. It always looks brand new, and I'm sure I've never seen a speck of dust on the thing.

"I had to ditch it, don't worry Myles will pick it up later. Get in."

"This thing is filthy."

"It's a classic GMC pickup, you should be proud to ride in it. Get in before I throw you in." He threatened back to his foul mood and meanness.

I wiped who knows what from the seat to the floor and climbed in. "We have enough money to buy a decent form of transportation."

He slammed the door and walked around to sit in the driver's seat. All this door slamming needs to stop, it's making me jumpy.

"I would appreciate if you would not slam doors in my face." I scolded him as he started the poor old engine.

"I would appreciate if you would kindly shut the fuck up." He snapped and shoved the truck into gear. I gasped at his words then looked out the window figuring something had him in a mood, and I was not about to remain the target of his aggression.

A full five minutes later he said, "Sorry. It's been a long night."

"You didn't sleep?"

"Not much. I woke up about an hour after you fell asleep and went to deal with the car bullshit."

"Lou. Language please?" I interrupted as nicely as I could.

He glanced at me, "Lighten up Barbie. Are you hungry?"

I sighed once again forcing myself to resign to my situation. "Yes, breakfast would be nice."

"I know a diner in New Bern you should like."

"What makes you say I should like it?"

"They have grits."

I laughed for the first time since this ordeal began. "You have me there Mr. Colson. I do love good grits."

"There, we have one thing in common."

"Two." I corrected him.

He looked at me again, "Two? What's the other thing?"

"We both need a haircut."

He pretended to give me a dirty look but the way his mouth turned up at the corners gave away his amusement. "I'm growing it back out, if you must know. It just happens to be at a weird length. Joe said I looked like Johnny Depp."

"No, he's much shorter, and if I remember correctly you have blue eyes and he has brown."

"You sound as if you've met the man." He suggested.

"Briefly. More like a passing introduction at an event. I've been introduced to many famous people, however I can't say as I know them." I explained.

"You talk like music." He replied looking to his left.

"Pardon me?"

"Nothing." He fumbled with the radio for a minute before pretending to care about the news more than talking to me. We talked on and off about various topics. Agreeing to disagree on some things came fairly easily as I didn't wish to rouse up that foul mood again. I'm sure we could have a good go-around over our differences, but not today. I'd rather save that sparring for a happier occasion. Maybe once this is over I'll have to put together a party. Invite Lou. Thank him.

I smiled and shook my head. He'd never show up. Funny, but I find myself liking that about him.

"What's so funny?"

"Nothing really."

"If it was nothing, you wouldn't have laughed. Tell me what's funny." He insisted blowing his hair out of his eyes.

"Well, if I must be honest, I was trying to imagine you in a suit."

"The only suit you'll see me in will be on my wedding day, and that's not about to happen anytime soon."

"I'm sure your girlfriend is thrilled."

"Girlfriend?? Ha!" He said that a little too loud making me jump. Realizing his mistake he apologized, "Sorry honey. It's just the mere idea of having a girlfriend sets me off. My job doesn't leave much room for relationships."

"Somehow I doubt it's your job that's the problem." Okay, I seriously need too filter myself.

"Oh really? And just what do you think, in your professional opinion, is my problem?"

"You're rude, grabby, and up until last night, you stunk."

He cracked up. "I stunk. Very nice Barbie. Very nice."

"Just drive." I turned the volume up on the crackling advertisement. Of course there's no music playing to at least attempt to cover my obvious discomfort. At least these jeans are comfortable. I miss my Jimmy Choos. The poor things are shoved carelessly into one of his bags.

Almost seven hours later, the sign reading Black Mountain perfectly described my mood, and added to my fear. "Where are you taking me?" I'm less afraid of Lou than I am the rest of this adventure. I don't know this man, and now I'm about to meet his brother. This Turner guy sounds dreadful. I can only hope his 'bitch', or 'old lady', as Lou insists on calling her, is nice. I could use someone to talk to right about now.

Normally that would be Myles. I miss my best friend. Lou is forcing me to realize just how much I take for granted when it comes to Myles. He really does spoil me. Lou does not spoil me. Not one bit.

"Where are you taking me?"

"Wherever I see fit to keep you alive." There's that bad mood again. It seems the longer we go without speaking, the snippier he gets when I break the silence. This man is either a jerk, or complicated. I'm going with jerk at the moment.

"I just asked where we are going, no need to get snippy."

"I don't get 'snippy', I get annoyed. The last transport that mouthed off to me found himself in the fucking trunk. Don't think you're any different just because you wear a damn skirt."

I can't believe the audacity of this man!! Instead of dignifying him with a reply I un-dignified myself with a good pout out the window. The man is unbearable. I can't wait for this to be over. I hope my father is okay . . . shoot. What if he's not?? Then what do I do?? I've been so busy being mad at this jerk next to me I haven't had time to worry about my father.

Lou picked up my hand so I looked at him. His expression had softened, "It's going to be okay. I won't let anything happen to you."

I snatched my hand back, "I can take care of myself thank you Mr. Colson. You are, if nothing else, a hinderance. Kindly give me my father's money and drop me somewhere with a public telephone. I've had enough of your mouth."

He slammed on the brakes making me brace myself with my hands on the dashboard. Then he grabbed my arm to face him. "I'm not here to be nice, or cater to your every snobbish desire like Myles. Me being here is a risk I rarely take. Anywhere east of the Mississippi river is an invitation to get a lot of people hurt. People I love. I don't give a rat's ass about you beyond keeping you alive and getting paid. Now sit back and for once today, shut the hell up." He let go and pulled back onto the now dirt road. "Women." I heard him complain as I composed myself.

"Insufferable ass." I went back to looking out the window.

"You call me insufferable. I've never met more stuck up bitch in my life." He informed me as he sped up.

"Probably because you hang around loose women." Great, now I'm picking fights with this man. This man I barely know.

"As a matter a fact, I do not. Although I did get a wicked forty-dollar blow job before I left Arizona."

I covered my ears, "I did NOT need to know that!!"

He's laughing now. "Yeah, probably not, but you're irritating the shit out of me."

"Maybe we shouldn't speak to each other for a while." I suggested firmly.

"Good idea." I can see him shaking his head. "You talk too much anyway."

"I was trying to be polite." I argued.

"And she's still talking." He glanced at me. "You don't get out much, do you?"

I crossed my arms over my chest. "I get out plenty Mr. Colson."

"Boyfriend take you out to fancy restaurants and shit?"

"Language Mr. Colson." I reminded him before continuing. "No, I'm currently between boyfriends." I lied. I've never had a boyfriend. I've played spin the bottle type games over the years, but aside from an uncomfortable sloppy kiss here and there, my experience with men is very limited.

"No wonder you're so uptight."

"Pardon me??"

He looked over to me as he slowed for yet another turn, "You need to get laid. Don't worry, Im not picking on you. I could use a good fuck myself."

My face went bright red, "We need to stop talking."

He laughed, "I tried telling you that."

2

A little while later he finally stopped at what might as well have been an outhouse in the middle of nowhere. When he started covering the truck with random branches I decided to try and help.

"How long before your brother gets here?" I asked hoping my tone wasn't going to set him off again. He's quite scary when he's mad.

"Maybe an hour or so." He shrugged.

"Where did you get this truck?"

"I stole it."

"Then you should give it back."

"I'll send someone back for it later."

This surprised me. "You will?"

"Sure. I try to borrow more than I steal, but sometimes shit doesn't work out. This truck shouldn't be a problem to return to it's owner in a week or so."

"I hope so. I know you're just doing your job, but I'm not partial to thievery."

"Neither am I. I am however partial to getting my job done and collecting a paycheck." He informed me as he tossed a large branch over the hood of the truck. He's obviously very strong, and moves with a confident grace. This is a man who is comfortable in his own skin. It made me wonder if I'm as confident. No, probably not.

"What do we do now?" I asked trying to hide the driver's side mirror with smaller branches.

"We're going to walk back to the main road a couple miles back, that way Turner won't have to bring Daisy all the way up here."

"Daisy? Is that his wife?"

"No, that's his rig. Georgia is his old lady."

"Old lady? I've heard this term before, but never really understood why you would refer to your significant other as 'old lady'."

"Yeah, seems my big dumb brother found himself a woman. First Joe, now Turner. Somebody must have tilted the world on it's axis, because that's some shit I never saw happening. Especially Turner. That man ain't right. Any woman brave enough to put up with him is alright in my book, or just as crazy as he is."

"What about you?" I asked as we started walking. "Do you ever think about having an old lady?"

"No. I am happily single." He shifted his bags to one hand after hefting a large backpack over his shoulder.

"Oh, right, the whore." I remembered his rude and disgusting comment about a certain sexual act in Arizona before the conversation got too personal for comfort.

"Actually, that was a rare moment. It had been a while and I was in more of a physical need than an emotional need. Don't think poorly of all whores Barbie. Ginger is a professional, and takes her job very seriously. All the girls do." Just because I don't sleep with the paid ladies, doesn't mean I don't respect what they do.

"I just can't imagine the diseases."

"No diseases. Stacy is their Madam, she makes sure they use protection and get checked out by a doctor once a month, or whatever it is. I don't exactly know the details, but I know Stacy runs a tight ship. They are very attractive and well kept ladies. The only reason I gave in to Ginger was because she'd been flirting with me for the last week. Everyone knows I don't sleep with the ladies of the night, so I guess she saw it as a challenge. I guess we both won." He explained rather easily.

"I'm not sure how to reply to that."

"Then don't. You asked, so I answered. I don't have time to date Barbie. It's been almost three years since my last serious relationship, that's a long time for a man." He hinted.

"I honestly wouldn't know, but I suppose for a man that is a long time. I apologize for misjudging you."

"I don't care. Whatever you think of me doesn't mean shit. When this is over you can go back to your big southern mansion, and your fancy high heels. I'll go back to my club and pick up another job. I'm sure we'll both be very happy to be done with each other."

"I'm sure you're right Mr. Colson." I agreed hoping to put an end to this before it becomes more bickering.

We walked in silence for a while before he pointed to a large recreational vehicle coming towards us. "That's Daisy. I should warn you, Turner is a huge asshole. He doesn't speak to anyone except me via hand signals. Just stay out of his way, and whatever you do, do not pick a fight with him like you do me. He'll toss us both out of a moving vehicle if he sees fit."

"Sounds scary."

"Very. Turner and I do some jobs together now and again. His toys are very helpful, and he's armed to the gills. Like I said, hang back, and keep that sassy little mouth of yours shut."

"Sassy?"

He stopped walking as the RV pulled over to the side of the narrow dirt road and turned to look at me. Cool blue eyes locked onto mine. "This is dangerous territory for all of us. I need you do exactly what I tell you, got it?"

"Geeze, calm down."

"I asked you a question." He pushed.

"Yes, I get it." Now he's riling me up again. I need to breathe and try to calm down before I say something rude.

"Good." He let go and stood upright to greet the giant man with long blonde hair who stepped down from the RV. They shook hands and did that man-hug thing guys do. "Hey Bro. Good to see you."

The large man nodded and reached around behind him.

A nice looking woman in horrible clothing came around and held her hand out to Lou. "Hi, I'm Georgia."

Lou shook her hand, "Lou, but you knew that from the texts." He motioned to me, "This is my charge, Barbie."

I held my hand out to meet hers, "Barbara, please. Nice to meet you Georgia."

"You too. I'm so glad to have another woman to talk to! Come inside. Are you hungry? Thirsty?"

"Both, yes. Thank you Georgia." I followed her inside making sure to give Lou a nice long dirty look along the way. Why couldn't he be this nice?

The RV is huge, and gorgeous. Various beige fabrics and matching leather. Everything smells new. I sat at the table and scooted toward the window so I wasn't in the way.

Georgia sat across from me with wine and a plate of cheese, fruit, and crackers. She started opening the wine as the guys entered through the same door we'd come through. I caught Turner giving Georgia an awfully dirty look, not much different from the one I'd given Lou.

She stuck her tongue out at him and said, "Forget it Turner. I haven't spoken to another woman in weeks. I'm talking to this one."

I heard him growl low in his throat so I looked at her, "Is he mad?"

She shrugged, "He's always mad, just ignore him. Don't get me wrong, he's a good man, just not housebroken, and very rude. Like I said, ignore him."

"I shall do just that. Have you been together long?"

"A few weeks. He kind of kidnapped me, but then I fell in love with him, so here we are." She shrugged.

"Kidnapped you??" I was shocked.

"Sort of. I had just lost a case because a client lied to me. I was humiliated in court, and decided to go get drunk with some old friends. Old friends I owed a debt to. Turner decided to collect on his own debt with Slider, the guy I owed the debt to. He took me as payment for said debt. Since I owed Slider basically my life, I couldn't say much when he approved the deal."

"What debt could you possibly owe to someone that would warrant you being kidnapped??"

"To make a long story short he saved my life. The real problem is that it cost a dear friend of his his life in the end. A life for a life if you will. I'm not sure what the debt was that Slider owed Turner. I've been afraid to ask."

"That sounds horrible! Who is this Slider?"

"He's the President of the club. The motorcycle club known as Exiles. The main chapter is in Arizona, but there are a ton of chapters that reside under the Exiles umbrella."

"I'm so confused." I sipped the wine. It's good.

She laughed. "Let me try that again. A chapter is a group of like-minded bikers. They go on runs, charity events, all kinds of things. If an outside chapter wants they can apply to be part of the club. The club is Exiles, but each chapter has it's own name." She got up and held a large black leather jacket up to show me.

She pointed to the patch in the center. "Turner is Exiles, but he's Nomad, which means he doesn't hang out at one particular chapter. If you belong to a chapter your city or state goes down here, and the name of your chapter up here."

She turned the jacket to show me the side, "If Turner was part of a chapter instead of being Nomad the name of that club would go here, and the chapter name here." She pointed back to the 'Exiles' patch on the top of the back. "Since Turner is part of the club, and has a pretty high ranking status with his brother being the club president, he wears Exiles like they are his chapter. In a way they are, but he's never there, so he's considered Nomad." She pointed to the word written, or I should say sewn, into the bottom under the intimidating logo.

"Oh. Okay." I think I'm starting to understand.

"It's different for different clubs. Some clubs want their name on every jacket where our chapter names are now. Those are the clubs that practice patch-overs. Slider changed things up years ago so the chapters could retain their original names. He said something about wanting to preserve the heritage of the chapters. I guess he's into history." She shrugged.

"So . . . Exiles is the main chapter, and the club name?"

"Yes."

"And there are chapters all over that belong to his club?"

"Yes."

"What is the point of all this?"

"It's a brotherhood, a family. They take care of each other, trust each other. Slider has certain rules he enforces to keep the club as respectable as possible. We have our bad apples just like everyone else, but they deal with it in-house. If a chapter breaks too many rules, they get punished and eventually booted out of the club if Slider sees fit."

"How long has this club been around?"

"I think Slider's father, Bull, started it in California in around 1940, but I'm not sure. When Slider took over years ago he moved it to Apache Junction. He likes the mountains in Arizona better I guess. That's what his wife, Salina, says anyway."

"Is Lou a member?"

She leaned over, "Hey Lou?"

"Yes ma'am?"

"Are you nomad?"

"No, I'm out of Washington, just outside Seattle, the Newcastle chapter. General's Tribe."

She looked back to me, "There's a main chapter for each state, and a bunch of city chapters under that." She leaned over to ask Lou. "Is General's Tribe the Washington hub?"

His voice came from behind me, "Nah, just a small chapter in the suburbs. Mostly weekend warriors and charity runs for kids."

"Thank you Lou. Turner, stop glaring at me before I kick you." She shook her head and rolled her eyes before looking back to me. "Anyway, being part of the main chapter for a state is kind of a big deal for the guys. The smaller chapters, like Lou's, are more my style. The one we're going to, the main one for the entire club, is pretty big. When they have rallies they have to rent entire fields."

"Wow. That's quite a big deal."

"Yes, it is. My family has always run tight with the chapter, so a lot of my friends hang out there. Now for the complicated part." She sipped her wine giving me a second to catch up.

"Slider is the oldest of twelve blood brothers. There are untold half brothers. Lou is a half brother, and Turner is a full blood brother to Slider. Their father was intent on having many, many sons. Anyway, all the guys refer to each other as 'brothers', so it can be a little confusing."

"I'm glad you said something, I might have started to think they were all related." I laughed at my ignorance.

"They might as well be, but you can tell the Colson brothers from the rest pretty easily. They're all big as houses."

"Turner is the biggest man I've ever seen. When he stepped inside the room suddenly became very small." I cringed a little.

She laughed as she complained "Yeah, try sleeping with him."

I blushed and looked away to sip my wine.

"What do you do Barbara?" She thankfully changed the subject.

"I work for my father, sort of. He travels all over making business deals I know very little about. Since finishing college I've been back at the plantation keeping the books. It was something to do while I figured out what I wanted to do with my life. It's all rather boring to be honest, but it's nice to be home for a change. Or was." I looked down at my glass.

"You'll get back soon. This rig is like a tank, we should be pretty safe in the meantime." She sounded so sure I believed her. She's much nicer company than Lou with his piercing blue eyes and drastic moods swings.

"It looks like any other fancy RV."

"I think she's mostly bullet proof, and there's a main computer that talks, so if you hear her don't freak out."

"Oh wow, it's amazing what they can do with technology these days." I looked around still not seeing anything out of ordinary.

"Yes it is. I think Turner's brother Joe worked with him to design and build her. It takes a little getting used to, but she's pretty cool."

"Does this Joe like to dress his girlfriend like hobos too?" I laughed lifting the hem of my shirt a little.

She laughed with me, "Oh my God! I know right! I can't wait to go shopping. Turner didn't exactly give me a chance to pack, so I've resorted to wearing his clothes, or mine between washings. Trust me, the first chance I get, I'm going to Dillards."

"I'll be right there with you." I promised.

"It's a date!"

Lou's voice came from behind us, "Will you two stop talking about us like we're not here?"

"No." I decided. "Talking about someone behind their back is rude." I schooled him.

Georgia smiled really big and got up. "Come on, we'll go in the back and watch a movie." She picked up a throw pillow and threw it at Turner so it bounced off his shoulder. Turner picked it up and chucked it back at her.

She caught it and set it aside. "One of these days I'm going to kiss that dirty look of his face."

"Why does he look at you so mean?" I asked as we sat on the bed.

"He's a very private person. Me talking to you like this is killing him. I think it's funny as hell after what he's put me through lately."

"Put you through?"

She rolled her eyes and looked at me, "Turner has a warped sense of humor. He took me camping for a while at first. We were roughing it like nobody's business. We had quite a few ugly arguments, then out of the blue he decides to show me his fancy mansion buried deeper in the mountains. I wanted to shoot him." She started sifting through a library of DVD's on a shelf.

"By the way, we have guns stashed all over, so if you flip a pillow over, like that one behind you, and there's a handgun, don't be surprised."

"I'll keep that in mind. Do you shoot?"

"I do. You?"

"I'm an excellent shot. I have seventeen marksmanship medals and for the last few years I've been teaching courses in gun safety at the college." I boasted like a fool. Thankfully she looked past my egotistical slip.

"Oh cool!!" We talked more than not through the movie. It was nice to take my mind off things for a while.

Later that evening, when we finally stopped for the night, Lou insisted on irritating me in every way possible. Georgia saw that he was egging me on just to get a rise out of me, and therefore found us amusing. Turner however, did not find us the least bit amusing. He glared at Lou more than once. I tried my best to ignore Lou, but he's fixated on my being a delicate southern belle who couldn't find her way out of a wet paper bag.

Later, after Turner took Georgia to the back room for what I'm assuming is a rant of silence about his current situation, I caught on to what Lou was doing to the living space for our bedding. "I am *not* sleeping in the same bed with you again tonight!" I almost yelled again. This man is dancing on my last nerve.

"Yes, you are. We can't block the aisle." He fluffed a pillow and patted it. "Come on Barbie, I won't bite."

"I'll sleep in the chair."

"No, you're going to sleep right here, where I can keep an eye on you. I don't trust you not to get up and go for walk in the middle of the night. Or something stupid like that." He pointed to the bed. "Come on beautiful. I'm tired, you're tired, and tomorrow is only going to be another long day."

"No. I refuse to sleep with you. And if it's another long day, it's because you have chosen to irritate me at every turn." I crossed my arms in defiance.

The door opened from behind me and before I could react Turner grabbed me around the waist and thrust me onto the mattress. Lou quickly blocked my escape. "Thanks bro."

The door was closed immediately behind Turner as he went right back to the bedroom. That man is scary.

I looked at Lou, "You are the most insufferable, pain in my a . . . arse." I gave up and laid down with my back to him.

He pulled a blanket over me and got elbowed when he put his arm around me next. "Oof. Nice hit Barbie."

"Stop calling me that."

"Barbie Barbie Barbie." He sang in my ear.

I swatted him away like a fly. "Stop that."

He's shaking as he laughs behind me. "Goodnight kitten."

"What did you call me?"

"Kitten. You have cute little claws for such a fluffy little southern lady."

I laughed, "I am not fluffy!"

"Oh yes you are, fluffy and soft. Your skin is like white rose pedals, and you have the best curves."

"Don't talk about my curves. I've had a weight problem my entire life. I hate my curves."

"Oh no honey, you have great curves." He put his hand on my hip. "Men like curves, gives them a place to put their hands."

I smacked his hand, "Kindly unhand me."

He put it back around my middle and hugged me to his chest. "Goodnight kitten."

I groaned but couldn't find it in me to fight any longer. "Goodnight Mr. Colson."

When I woke up it was because there was a very heavy man laying on top of me snoring in my ear.

"Lou! Wake up!" I whisper-yelled trying to push him off of me.

He groaned, "Nooo, I don't want to go to school."

I laughed because it's obvious he's awake and trying to be funny. "You have to go to school, so you can learn some manners. Now move, you're squashing me."

He lifted up and looked down at me with sleepy sweet light blue eyes, "How do you wake up more beautiful than when you went to sleep?"

I think my heart just imploded. What did he just say??

He kissed the end of my nose and hopped off. "I get the bathroom first."

I had to blink and shake my head a couple times as I sat up. That man is not right. How can he be so insufferable one minute, then tell me I'm beautiful the next??

Georgia fixed us all a breakfast of eggs, bacon, and pancakes a little while later. I offered to help, but she sweetly declined based only on the lack of room to move around in the limited working space of the kitchen. I decided to talk to her from the table to keep her company. Otherwise I'm stuck talking to Lou, and he's just plain baffling to me at the moment. When he came out of the bathroom earlier he'd given me this long appraising look that lingered much longer than it should have. It's like there's something going on in that man's head he's struggling with. I wish he'd figure it out and stop messing with my head already.

Over breakfast I kept catching Lou looking at me. He'd look away quickly pretending it was an accident, but I can feel his eyes on me when he looks. Now I get it. He's trying to decide if he wants to seduce me. I've seen this look before.

I tend to scare men off with my coolness and impeccable grammar. Maybe it's not impeccable, but it's definitely off-putting to men trying to get laid. I'm a lady, not some tool to be used for a man's pleasure.

Now we're back on the road. The day is long and boring, so Georgia and I decided around four o'clock in the afternoon to go in the back and watch another movie over a bottle of wine. Turner and Lou had exchanged some sort of communication via hand signals that were somewhat like traditional sign language, but not so close that I could understand completely. I did manage to pick up that he refers to her as his peach. I guess the big guy has a soft spot after all.

Just before she got the DVD in the player we heard some loud whacks hit the back of the RV. That was no nail, and it definitely wasn't a pot hole. I know guns, and those are bullets trying to get through to us.

When Georgia grabbed her gun from a drawer, I went for the one under the pillow she'd shown me yesterday.

I stumbled once as I jumped up on the bed and kicked the screen from the window before leaning out. Georgia is now in the living room shooting from behind me.

Together we took out a pickup truck and two armed men on motorcycles. I hated shooting at the men on the bikes even though they were shooting at us.

Georgia might have gotten another rider, but I couldn't be sure as I was suddenly jerked from the window and tossed to the floor. I rolled to my side and looked around. Lou and his brother Turner are firing back now. I looked up the hall to see Georgia is also on the floor a few feet away.

She smiled at me and gave me a thumbs up. "Nice shooting!!"

"You too!" I felt a bond form between us. We've done battle together. We'll be friends for life.

We both got our butts royally chewed out when the guys stopped to investigate the damage to the RV a little while later.

Georgia looked particularly disheveled when we saw each other again. Turner had slammed the door to the bedroom when he'd lit into her. I couldn't hear him, but I could hear her. she gave as good as she got from what I could tell. I get the feeling she can read his mind, which is probably his undoing. I almost feel sorry for him. Almost. He's still a huge jerk.

"Are you okay?" I asked her when she emerged from the back bedroom a while later. Lou had given up scolding me and took on a full blown pout a few feet away.

"Oh yeah. he's just very protective, and I scared the shit out of him." She hopped up on her tip toes to reach for something from the top shelf over the fridge. Her shirt came up a little and I saw a few bruises on her hip.

"Did you get those today?" I nodded to her midriff when she looked at me.

She looked down and smiled, "It's not as bad as it looks."

"It looks like it hurts. Are you sure you're okay?"

"Of course. If he actually hurt me I'd kill him. He's not *trying* to bruise me Barbara. He just gets carried away. I think love does that to a man."

"I would think love would make a man more careful." I argued.

"In Turner's case, love has made him more passionate. He gets carried away, but he'd never hurt me. All I have to do is tell him to chill and he does. The problem is, I like his passion. Like I said, the bruises look worse than they really are." She assured me.

The next two days we lived together uncomfortably. Georgia and I were fine, but I've developed a loathing for Turner. It must have been obvious because Lou even stopped bickering with me so much. I think he felt sorry for me.

When they dropped us off at the club, which looked more like a military compound, I couldn't have been more relieved. Turner must have been too because they didn't even get out of the RV before leaving again.

Lou put his arm around my shoulders and introduced me to a few of the guys. I remember Goat, but that's about it. Once inside what I now know is a biker bar, he ordered us a couple drinks from the bartender who has beautiful long red hair. I envy hair like that. Mine is mousy brown and quite boring, as am I.

Lou pulled my chair out for me so I sat looking around. "It feels like a very well kept antique store in here."

"Red likes her antiques. Poor Joe, the guy went from Marine slash Navy Seal to baby-making pack mule. He's always dragging something home she's bought."

He laughed and I felt a bit of relief. Lou has a very nice laugh, it's not very loud, but it's honest.

"I bet he's very happy, she's a beautiful young lady. I wish I had hair like that." I admitted before sipping my beer directly from the bottle. Usually I pour it into a glass, but that seems overkill here.

"It's hard to tell, the man's a rock, like Turner."

"Turner is an ass. Excuse my language, but that man is just plain mean. Did you hear the way Georgia screamed?"

He laughed, "Those were not screams of agony kitten, those were pleasure screams. Lucky fucking bastard." He looked at me, "Sorry."

"I'll accept your apology, as the subject bothers me so. Why do you say lucky??" I asked suddenly realizing what he was saying.

He smirked, "The more noise you can get from a woman the more you know she's enjoying herself."

I blushed and felt a rush of butterflies in my belly. I don't know anything about physical pleasure with a man. I've spent my life in prep school or hanging out with bodyguards.

"Are you turning red?" he leaned in to look at me, "Aw, the ballsy little southern belle is blushing?"

"Stop teasing me, it's not funny. You say the crudest things." I tried to hide what I knew was my very red face by taking a drink of my beer and turning to look elsewhere.

He took my hand and put it under his on the table as the redhead appeared. "Hey Red. This is my charge Barbie. Barbie, this is Red. You got any good eats tonight?"

"The usual." She smiled at me after seeing our hands on the table. I tried to pull away, but Lou has a good grip. "You want pasta or Mexican?"

Lou looked at me, "You decide."

I smiled up at her. "Can we have one of each and a couple extra plates?"

She beamed, "Sure. Two more beers?"

"And a SoCo back." I added.

She winked, "You got it babe. Welcome to the club." She twirled on one toe and left us alone.

I looked at Lou who is looking at me like I've lost grown a second head. "What?"

"SoCo back? Who are you? First you escape handcuffs, then you shoot like a pro, now you drink like one?"

I felt my mouth curve up into a smile betraying my amusement at his surprise. "There are many things you don't know about me Mr. Colson."

He narrowed his eyes and sat back keeping my hand but moving it to his knee. "The handcuffs I figure Myles taught you. He teach you to shoot too?"

"At first, yes. Then I took some classes, entered a couple competitions, and before I know it I have seventeen various awards from tournaments. Skeet is my favorite."

His eyebrows went straight up like they were attached to strings. "Are you serious?"

I nodded taking another drink before saying. "Yes. Last year I wanted to donate some local turkeys for Thanksgiving to the orphanages around town. I threw a hunting party for all the employees working the plantation. Those who didn't hunt helped with the event. It was quite a turn out, I'd like to do it every year."

"People still use the word 'plantation'?"

"It is what it is Lou, I can't change the name of the place. Not yet anyway." I thought about my father.

"Did you hunt?" Lou asked going back to the original topic of conversation.

Feeling sure of myself again, in a conversation I am comfortable with I replied with pride, "Oh yes, I shot three turkeys, we took twenty three total, but that was after an all day hunt. Turkey hunting is tricky. You have to shoot all at once or they run before the rest of the hunting party can get off a shot. We use hand signals and turkey calls to communicate."

"Sounds like a fun day." He didn't sound convinced. I'm sure he would rather be on his motorcycle any day.

"Do you hunt Mr. Colson?"

"No. I'm the guy saving the hunted from being shot." He gave me a wink and a cocky smile.

I cringed, "Makes me look like the bad guy."

Red saved him from replying by setting down two casserole dishes and two plates. "Lasagna, the house fav, and enchiladas. "The enchiladas are fresh from the oven. I had to reheat the lasagna, but it's always best the second go around anyway. Anything else?" She asked as another server set our drinks down. I couldn't help but notice this female server is not wearing much in the way of clothing.

"This looks wonderful Red, thank you." I'm suddenly starving as the aroma of a fresh home cooked meal filled my nose.

"Okay, enjoy, and Lou, you should let go of the poor girl's hand so she can eat." She winked at him and left like before with that happy little twirl. She seems like a very happy person. I wonder what kind of man it takes to make a woman that happy.

Lou surprised me by kissing the back of my hand and batting those lashes at me. "I want this back later."

I pretended he hadn't just said and done that, and served up the lasagna first when he let go of my hand.

"Thank you." He said as I put food on his plate.

"You're welcome. Do you know how my father is?" I asked wondering if he'd been in contact with anyone recently.

"Yes, he's fine for now. I don't know where they're hiding him though. Sorry." He took a big bite, looking as hungry as I am.

We ate like starving idiots before finally sitting back with the second beers.

I put my hand over my stomach. "I believe Red is a fabulous cook. If I hang around here too long I'll be right back into a larger dress size."

He smiled and leaned over to take my hand back. "Tomorrow we head north."

"North?"

"Yeah, I'll tell you later in case you get drunk and start running off at the mouth."

I remembered my Southern Comfort and picked it up taking a small sip. "Two shots will not have me drunk, of this I can assure you."

He laughed and kissed the back of my hand again, "You and your perfect little southern accent to go along with that smooth Southern Comfort. I have to admit the accent is very sexy." He sipped his beer and thanked the barely clad server for taking the plates away.

"I'm not sure how to respond to that." I laughed feeling the effect of the liquor as I take another sip and the music started. Nice. I like live music. I like music in general.

Lou leaned over and pulled my chair closer to his, I'm assuming so we can see the stage better. Then he leaned into my ear, which tickled, "Do you like to dance Miss Whitmore?"

"No, not the kind of dancing one would do in here." I replied eyeing the pole in the middle of the dance floor & turning my head towards his voice out of habit. His lips are way too close to mine.

His eyes danced on mine as he asked so only we could hear. "How about a walk outside then?"

I nodded, "That would be nice."

He kept my hand in his as we exited the building.

"Don't we need to pay the bill?" I asked not wanting to stiff Red after she'd gone through all the trouble to make such wonderful dishes.

"No, I have a running tab. She's still up a a few bucks."

"Up?"

"In the black. She tells me when the money runs out, and I drop her about three hundred. Saves me a lot of time when I come through town, which seems to be more often than not lately."

"Makes sense. Why are you holding my hand?" I asked as we walked along the row of motorcycles. They're quite beautiful machines, and all lined up like this they appear to be on display for a show.

"I like the way you feel. You have soft skin." He said simply.

"I'm afraid you're sending some very confusing signals Mr. Colson."

He was quiet for a minute until we stopped at the fence. Then he turned and lifted my chin. His eyes are still blue even in the dark. He ran his thumb over my cheek. "Your boyfriend is a very lucky man."

I laughed nervously and tried to look away from those bright blue eyes that seem to put me in a trance when I look into them for a second too long, "No boyfriend."

He looked confused, "How is that possible? You're beautiful, smart, and just sassy enough to make a man wonder what's under this soft skin of yours."

I gasped a little at his words. "I . . . don't have time."

"I find that hard to believe Miss Whitmore." He accused.

"I went to an all girls school until college. Once there I spent my time studying. Having a body guard hanging over your shoulder all the time doesn't help." I confessed.

"Are you telling me you've never had a boyfriend??" He looks confused now.

"Yes, that is precisely what I am telling you."

"But you've been kissed at a college party or something, right?"

I laughed again, "No. I didn't get invited to parties like those."

He almost looks like he's in pain as he looks at my mouth and runs his thumb over my lower lip. "Never been kissed?"

I shook my head afraid to speak.

He closed his eyes and dropped his forehead to mine. "If only I was a better man."

I gripped his leather vest because he'd leaned far enough into me that it knocked me a little off balance. "I never said you weren't a good man." I argued.

"Don't say that. I want to be your first kiss so bad it makes me a horrible man to want to soil such perfection and innocence."

"Why would you want me when there are much prettier and more experienced women inside?"

He stood upright still holding my chin, "You are a rare jewel kitten. The man that gets all your firsts is one lucky man. I hope he's smart enough to keep them only to himself."

"I . . . am once again struck speechless."

He smiled, "We should go in before I forget myself."

This time when he took my hand I didn't mind. Strange. "Where to now Mr. Colson?"

"There's an apartment available around back. I'll grab my bags and we'll go get some sleep. We should head out before noon tomorrow. I need some sleep."

"You didn't get enough sleep in the RV?" I asked curious since it seemed he was sleeping just fine to me.

"No. The only time I can sleep right is if I'm crashing at a clubhouse. Otherwise I sleep with one eye open."

"You seem to be sleeping pretty well when you're sprawled out all over me in the mornings." I accused.

"Looks can be deceiving." He let go of my hand to gather the bags from the ground beside the picnic table.

"Don't you worry about someone taking your things?"

"Not here. There are no thieves here, unless there's a practical joke involved."

I followed him around the side of the building and through a back door. He held the door open and flipped on a light switch. I was expecting a crappy cheap hotel type room, but this was very nice.

"Wow."

"Yeah, Red and Salina have been on a mission to clean up around here. This room used to be a storage area, now it's a second apartment."

"It's pretty without being too feminine. I like it." I opened the bag he'd given me for my new/old clothes after he set it on the bed.

He set the rest of the bags on the floor and fell onto his stomach across the bed. "Don't leave the room."

"And if I do?"

"You might get shot. Don't wander around here alone at night, it's dangerous for a stranger."

"They would kill me?"

"Not on purpose." He turned his head to look up at me. "But the snipers won't recognize you and the guys won't either. They'll hit on you, probably think you're one of the hang arounds."

"I don't know what that means."

"It means stay in the room." He grabbed a pillow and shoved it under his head.

"You're hogging the entire bed."

"Mm." And just like that, he was sound asleep.

I went through my nightly routine in a much better mood. The attached bathroom is larger than the one in the RV, but not by much. When I finished my nightly routine I went to stand over the bed looking at Lou.

He's long and lean, with strong broad shoulders and a fairly narrow waist. I walked around and worked his boots off. I doubt I can get his jacket off without waking him, so I curled up near him with a quilt I'd found on the back of an antique chair and fell soundly asleep with my back to him.

3

I woke to the sound of someone knocking on the door, "Room service!!" It sounds like Red.

I jumped up and opened the door, "Hi. Good morning." I fumbled half awake.

She smiled handing me a wicker basket. "Sorry for the rude awakening, but Lou asked for a wake-up call."

"Why didn't he set an alarm?" I asked not sure if I'm supposed to invite her in, or go out in the hall. Standing here in the doorway is uncomfortable.

She seemed to sense my tension and thumbed over her shoulder, "Coffee is behind the bar. Come help yourself after you wake the sleeping bear." She teased and started to retreat.

"Okay, I'll be right there. Thank you Red."

She waved and disappeared around the corner.

I closed the door and set the basket on the dresser. "Are you awake?"

He groaned and rolled over, "I am now."

"I'm going to go have coffee with Red while you wake up."

"Fine." He put his arm over his face like he might just go back to sleep instead.

As I'm in no hurry to spend the day in a vehicle with him again, I quickly grabbed his jacket, he must have taken if off during the night, because it's right here by the door and mine is on the chair across the room. I left in a hurry to find coffee and Red. I have a coffee addiction that must be addressed before I can function properly for the day. More than that, I'd like a minute to talk to Red before we leave.

Red saw me and looked over. "Have a seat, I'll pour. Cream and sugar?" She asked motioning to a table with a basket of muffins sitting in the center.

"Black, please. Did you do all this? It's so much fun to look around in here. A feast for the eyes if you will." I looked around the bar pulling the leather of Lou's over-sized around me to keep warm. It's a bit chilly in here and I'm glad I decided to steal his jacket as it covers more of my legs than my own.

"Salina and I did the decorating, Prospects did the labor."

I took the hot coffee. "Thank you."

She looked at me funny as she sat back with her coffee in hand.

"Is something wrong?"

"Why are you wearing that?" She nodded to Lou's jacket.

I looked down, "It was by the door and I felt the chill in the hall when I opened the door. Why? Will he be mad?"

"I doubt it since you don't know, but usually a man's cut is only worn by himself or his old lady. On the rare occasion he might use it to protect an unexpected passenger on their bike, but that's it. By wearing that you're saying you're his old lady."

I started to stand, "I'll go change."

She laughed, "Don't worry about it. I just thought you should know for future reference. It's not going to be a problem this once." She assured me and put her hand on my arm to keep me from getting up.

"I'll go take it off. I don't want to give anyone the wrong impression."

"No, don't do that. Leave it on. After seeing the way he was holding your hand last night, I can't wait to see his face with his cut on your back." She laughed.

I sat back in my chair, "This is such a different world than the one I'm used to."

She laughed and we proceeded to chat for a while getting to know each other. When I got to the part about Georgia and my concerns about her bruises she flew from her seat and disappeared through the door.

Before I could finish my coffee and go for another cup Red and two large men appeared in front of me.

The one with long greying hair and a patch that reads 'President' addressed me first. "How many bruises?"

"I didn't count, just a few on her hips and arms." I think my stomach is in my throat.

"Fuck!! That son of a bitch!!" He punched the air as he spun around angrily. "He knows I don't tolerate hurting women. Debt or no debt, he's going to answer for this."

"I don't think he means to." I tried to backpedal.

He spun on me, "I don't give a fuck if he meant to or not. My men do not hurt women. Period."

Lou stepped up and pulled me by his jacket back and behind him. "Easy bro. What's going on?"

"Turner is hurting Georgia?" Slider snapped at Lou.

"Not on purpose bro. You know him as well as I do, he's not . . . ."

"Fuck that. He knows the rules. Get out of here so I can bring him back in. If he finds out you two opened your traps he's going to want to kill you."

"Seriously bro . . . he doesn't . . . ."

"FUCK THAT!!" Slider yelled really loud this time making me jump about two feet straight up in the air, then left us standing there looking at the door that slammed behind him.

I looked up at Lou, "I'm so sorry."

He pulled me in for a hug holding my head against his chest. "It's okay kitten. Slider is just going to teach Turner a little lesson, that's all. Come on, let's get ready to go."

I started crying uncontrollably.

"Whoa." He hugged me tighter. "Easy baby. Easy. It's okay. You didn't do anything wrong."

"I feel like a shit! Georgia is going to hate me!"

He laughed and cupped my face to look into my eyes, "You did good kid. Relax. We're a family, we look out for each other. If Turner is going to take an old lady then she falls under our protection too. You didn't do anything I wasn't already thinking about doing. Okay?" He tried to reassure me.

I nodded, "I still feel bad."

"And I still feel like kissing you." He smacked my rear end. "Come on woman, let's go to Vegas."

"Las Vegas?"

"The one and only." He took my hand and pulled me towards the hall down to the apartment.

"Did you just smack me on the tush again?? I thought I told you that was not to happen again Mr. Colson." I scolded him, but my heart wasn't in it.

"You have a very spank-able ass Miss Whitmore." He replied.

"Language Lou." I scolded him.

He held the door for me. "Nag."

"I am not getting on that death trap." I stepped back crossing my arms in defiance.

He turned and grabbed me around the waist setting me on the rear seat of the large burgundy and chrome machine. "Yes, you are. We're back on my turf now. We ride." He insisted.

I'm sitting funny because the bike is resting on it's kickstand. My foot doesn't quite reach the ground so this balancing act is a little tricky. I ride horses Mr. Colson, not motorcycles."

He set a helmet on my head and fastened the chin strap. He gripped my jaw gently and looked into my eyes, "As long as I'm in charge, you do what I say. I'm going to get on in front of you. Put your arms around me and hold on tight."

"I'm going to die."

He rolled his eyes and smirked, "Not on my watch baby."

Baby?? Did he just call me baby?? My brain locked up at his words so all I could do is watch as he climbed on in front of me, righted the bike, then started the loud thundering engine.

He leaned back as he walked the large motorcycle back out of the parking space. "Put your arms around me Barbie!" He reminded me like I was a child who needed to be told one too many times to do something mundane.

I did as he instructed and hid my face in his back. God help me.

"Oh yeah, that's better. Tighter!" He yelled as he hit the gas and pulled onto the road.

I squeezed as hard as I could. I couldn't open my eyes until the first stop. Two women in the car next to us were looking Lou and the bike over, deliberately ignoring me.

My inner bitch reared her ugly head and sat straight up with me. I leaned forward into his ear. "Looks like you have a couple admirers."

He looked over and nodded, "Chicks loooove motorcycles baby!" He said it loud enough they could hear.

Oh good Lord, he's called me 'baby' again.

A couple turns later Lou's hand patted and rubbed my leg like he was trying to comfort me.

I tried to summon the strength to look up, but we're going so fast! It took some focus and determination not to wimp out before I finally found the courage to brave the wind and look up from his intimidating patch on the back of his jacket. Okay. I can do this.

"Relax! You need to trust me!" He yelled over his shoulder as he slowed for another turn.

I managed to lift my head and look up over his shoulder. Oh no. The freeway!! No!! I went back into hiding behind his back.

He laughed and drove us on two balanced wheels into fast moving traffic. Two wheels!! Horse have four legs to stay balanced. I'm going to die.

The first stop was Flagstaff. He pulled into a Harley dealership and helped me off the bike. "What are we doing here?"

"You need proper riding gear. Jeans and a flimsy leather jacket aren't enough, you need real leather." He informed me as we crossed the parking lot.

"Are you planning on crashing??"

He laughed, "No baby, you never plan on crashing, but you should always be prepared. The extra padding will keep you warm as we head further north. It's a lot cooler up there than down here in the desert." He opened the door for me.

I stepped inside and felt completely out of place. I turned and looked up at Lou, "Can't we just rent a car? I'll pay for it."

He rolled his eyes, "No baby, we can't. Come on, Julie over here will set you up."

"You know her?"

"She's a friend, sort of. I've run a couple jobs with her husband." He shrugged as he led me to this Julie.

Lou introduced us and gave her a list of items he wanted. A couple minutes later I was whisked away to the dressing room and handed various denim and leather items to try on.

I had to ask one too many times for help so Julie joined me in the dressing room. "You okay honey? You look scared out of your mind." She asked.

"I've never ridden a motorcycle before, it scares the dickens out of me."

She laughed, "Don't worry, you're with one of the best riders I know. He probably just wants to see you in all this sexy gear." She turned me to face the mirror. "What do you think?"

"Oh my. This is definitely out of my league. Who is that?" I pointed to the mirror where my reflection thinks she's some kind of bad ass biker chick.

Julie stepped back and looked me over, "Well honey, even if you are out of your element, you wear that leather like it was made for you. Lou is going to bust a nut when he sees this."

"A what?" I wasn't sure I heard her right.

"You'll see." She put her hand on the doorknob. "Ready?"

I took a deep breath and let it out slowly, "Okay, I think so."

She opened the door and stepped to the side. I looked up and saw Lou standing there with his hand over his mouth and a look of shock on his face. I think it's shock. I probably look ridiculous and he's laughing at me.

Then he strode forward making me step back into the dressing room. He pulled the door shut behind him and cupped my face. His blue eyes darkened as they looked into mine. "Oh honey, if you only knew what you do to me. I'm about to steal your first kiss." He warned me.

I was so relieved he wasn't laughing I nodded.

He touched his lips to mine twice before crashing into me and sinking his hands into my hair.

Oh my. This is kissing?? He's ravaging me!! Oh my. This is nice. My heart is pounding as he leads my tongue into a perfect dance with his. So this what the girls get all riled up about! No wonder they always look like giddy fools.

I put my arms around his neck so I don't fall as my knees weaken.

He took that as an invitation and moaned as his mouth took mine even harder and deeper. If this is anything like sex, I'm going to go into sensory overload and explode. Something is stirring in my belly. Butterflies. Lots and lots of butterflies.

He slowed and eased his way back to release and look at me, "I'm sorry. I couldn't help myself. You look so beautiful I lost my mind."

I smiled and tried to focus. "Don't be sorry. I don't know much about kissing, but I'm pretty sure that was wonderful."

He rested his palm on my my right cheek and ran his thumb over it as he looked at me. "We should go. Thank you for giving me your first kiss, I will never forget that one." He assured me before taking my hand and pulling me with him to pay the bill.

Once outside in the parking lot he got on the bike first this time and held his hand out for mine, "Swing your leg over, like riding a horse."

I hopped on my left foot twice before finding my place behind him.

He reached back and guided my arms back around his middle. "I like you here."

"What?" I asked unsure what he said. He started the engine and took off without replying. This man is getting weirder by the day. Wow. I just had my first kiss in the dressing room of a Harley dealership. I didn't see that one coming!

As a young girl I would dream of princes and first kisses under magnolia trees in the Spring. Flower petals flittered through the air as I imagined being swept off my feet by a gallant man in a white suit riding an equally gallant steed.

Well, he may not be gallant, but he's quite good at the kissing part. My lips feel swollen. Good thing he can't see me. I'm smiling like a school girl after being asked to the dance by the most popular boy in school. Although in this case I think I was just kissed by the bad boy in school. The one mothers warn their daughters about.

The scenery was not enough to keep me from resting my head on his back and closing my eyes. I'm tired for some reason. Lou has been an interesting distraction from worrying about my father, but now that we're riding I'm thinking too much. All this not knowing what's going on and why is frustrating to say the least. The worrying is exhausting. Traveling and meeting all these new people is also exhausting. Not to mention I didn't sleep too well last night. Evidently Lou snores when he's really getting a good night's sleep.

I sat up when I realized Lou was pulling over. He took us to the nearest hotel parking lot and helped me off.

"I think you've had enough. Sleeping on the back of my bike is a big no-no kitten."

"I'm sorry." I stifled a yawn. "I just feel so tired all of a sudden."

He scooped me up in his arms like a bride, "Yeah, I got that."

"I can walk Mr. Colson."

"We've shared a very passionate kiss kitten, you can call me Lou."

"I . . ."

"Don't know what to say? Yeah, I think I got that too." He pushed the lobby door open with his foot and walked right up to the counter. "I need a king and I need it now." He shifted and must have been going for his wallet. I hid my face in his shoulder completely mortified.

Five minutes later he's setting me on a large hotel bed and holding my chin. "Look at me."

I blinked trying to focus on disarming blue eyes, "Yes?"

"I'm going back to get the bike and get our shit. Can I trust you to stay put?"

"Yes. I don't have the energy to poot."

He laughed and tucked me under the covers. "So she does have a sense of humor. I think I'm in love." He smacked me on the butt. "I'll be right back."

"Hmm." Before he pulled the door shut behind him I was out cold. My last thought was of wishing I had the energy to tell him to stop smacking me on the rear, again.

I heard Lou talking and began to wake up. "She's fine Myles, just tired. Living with Turner and his old lady wore her out . . . Okay, ten a.m., no problem. Can you ride? . . . . Good. A prospect will meet you and bring you a bike. Meet us at the Luxor. Ask for Bret Colson and have them ring the room. We're borrowing my brother's penthouse suite. It comes with a security team and full surveillance system."

I sat up. Myles is coming to Vegas??

Lou saw me sitting up and came over to take my hand. "Do you know why he wants to meet with her? . . . . Alright. I'll see what I can find out on this end. Safe flight man." He hung up.

"Why is Myles coming to Las Vegas?"

He dropped to his knees in front of me and pushed his head to my stomach. "I don't know how to tell you this except to get it over with . . . your father has been killed."

I just sat there letting the words sink in. "How?"

He sat up taking my hands, "You don't want details. There's more."

"I'm listening." I felt the old teachings from prep school kick in. The Salem Academy For Girls teaches young ladies how to use their inner Salem Charm to push through any crisis. Let's hope I can do this.

"He wasn't your real father."

"What?"

"Your mother was pregnant when they met. He adopted you three days before your mother was killed."

"What the . . . ? I don't understand!!"

His eyes caught mine before the full panic attack set in. "Your real father is Paulie Marconni. He's one of the biggest mob enforcers in the country."

"How is that possible?"

"Your mother was one of his whor . . . girls. Back in those days it wasn't common knowledge that antibiotics and birth control don't mix, at least that's what Myles seems to think."

"My real father works for the mob??"

"Yes, and he wants to meet with you in Las Vegas."

"Why??"

"You just inherited over four billion dollars in cash and assets. He probably wants your money." He put his head down in my lap. "I'm sorry about your father."

"Which one? The distant money hungry liar? Or the criminal?" And here comes the anger part of mourning. That was fast.

Lou stood up and scooped me back into his arms. "Shower, food, then we need to go." He set me on the toilet with the lid closed and reached over to start the bath tub. "Hot or warm?"

"Warm." I replied automatically. My father is not my father, and now he's dead. My brain is processing his constant distance during my upbringing. He was absent at best.

I don't think he ever loved me, because I wasn't his, and he knew it. Shit. This really stinks. I've never felt so alone in my life. The weird part is, I've been alone all my life. Except for Myles. Suddenly I miss Myles so much my stomach hurts.

"How could my mother sleep with a mob boss?? Let alone be his whore."

Lou took my hand and looked me over, "Want some help?" He said it sweetly, not with sexual malice. He's trying to comfort me with his playfulness, and normally I might appreciate it, but not right now.

I managed a small smile, "No. Thank you Lou. I think I need a few minutes alone."

He lifted my chin, "Take your time, just don't fall asleep in the bathtub."

"Why did they kill him?" I looked up for his crystal blue eyes.

"I don't know sweetheart. Myles seems to think a business deal went bad and Paulie blames your father. He probably wants you to make up for whatever he lost now that you're rich."

"Now what do I do?" I feel so lost.

"When we get to Vegas Myles should have some more information. He's keeping me on the job until we're sure you're safe."

"I'm sorry. If you want out you can leave me to Myles. I'm sure he can take over for you."

"Absolutely not. Your father paid the club good money to keep you safe, and that's exactly what I plan to do." He kissed my forehead. "Take a nice long bath. I'm going to make some calls."

I was suddenly overwhelmed with the need for a hug so I lunged and latched onto him holding him tight. "Thank you." Tears filled my eyes and overflowed immediately.

He put his arms around me, "It's okay baby. I'm sorry about Mr. Whitmore. We'll figure this out, I promise."

I stepped back, "It's not that. I barely new my father. Now I know why. The whole thing is . . . crazy. I don't know how to deal with this."

"That's why you have me and Myles, we'll do everything we can to help you. Okay?" He's running his thumb over my cheek.

I nodded. "Thank you."

"Stop thanking me and take a bath." He kissed my forehead, and left. Suddenly the room felt empty and cold. I stripped down and got in the tub. I had to add more hot water to fully shake the chill that have been settling over me since I woke up. It made me think about what Red had told me about Lou's cut.

He hasn't said anything about finding me wearing it in the bar. Did he forget? Probably. Things have been pretty hectic. That's when I caught myself thinking too much about Lou when I really need to be focusing on my current problem.

Paulie Marconni. Sounds like an Italian pasta dish.

We rode up to Las Vegas after breakfast. I didn't eat much, my nerves are shot. Lou checked us into the Luxor under that Bret guy's name. I guess he's another brother.

I can't think straight enough to process Lou's extensive family.

"Here we go baby." Lou handed me a room key and an elevator key after we checked in. "In case I lose mine or you need it for any reason." He put his arm around my shoulders.

"When will Myles be here?"

"About two hours. Want to gamble after we unpack?" He asked obviously trying to distract me.

"No. I think I want to make some calls back home. The house needs to know about my father's death. Mr. Laraby is going to have to take over the books since I'm not sure how long I'll be gone. I need to call the family lawyer too."

"No problem." He held the elevator door for me. "I'm going to try calling Paulie again."

"Myles said Paulie wants to meet with me right?" I asked him trying to focus. Everything feels so unreal, like I'm watching my life from the front row of a movie theater. Things like this do not happen to boring women like myself.

"Yes, but it could be a trap honey. That's why I want to speak with him first. He's probably not returning my calls because he doesn't realize I'm in on this job."

"Was it Paulie who shot at us in the RV??" I can't believe I didn't ask this before.

"Possibly, but not likely. That was probably Turner's twin sister. Those two have been exchanging punches forever. I doubt she was after you, she most likely just wanted to put a couple bullets in the RV to tell him to get out of her territory."

"Why would she do that?"

"Turner likes to go back into her territory to screw with her. Last time he stole all the petcocks from her collection of bikes, then bought up every one for a hundred miles. I thought it was pretty funny, but I think she's still pissed."

"What is a petcock?"

"It's a valve that controls fuel to the carburetor on older bikes. Chardonnay loves old bikes. Anyway, it's been an old joke that we bikers forget to 'turn the gas on'. The first year I was riding I had a piece of tape on my handlebars that read 'Turn the gas on dipshit'. Anyway, if you remove the valve the engine doesn't get fuel, so it doesn't run."

"Oh. That was a very nice explanation, minus the language. We really do need to work on that filthy mouth of yours."

He ran his thumb along my jaw. The gesture and sweet compassionate look in his eyes held me frozen in place. "You could use yours to clean mine." He suggested with a quick smile that told me he was distracting me again. Although I get the feeling if this was a better place and time he might have kissed me. Would I have let him? Interesting question I cannot deal with right this moment.

He motioned for me to step out of the elevator and into a very large room. A very fancy room. It reminds me of the library at home with all the rich reds and warm browns. "This is the Tower Premiere Suite, Bret owns the entire floor, so we're alone except for security."

"Wow, this is really nice." There's a large dining table, a living area, a good sized kitchen, and a bedroom with a huge king size bed. I like that there are doors separating the bedroom from the living space. Maybe I can sleep alone for a change. The thought suddenly depressed me. That's weird. Will I miss Lou's big warm . . . safe, and now comforting body wrapped around mine every morning?

His voice snapped me back to the here and now. "Excuse me honey, that's Myles." He answered his phone, "Hey buddy, you're here already? . . . Good. I left instructions at the front desk, come on up." He hung up. "Looks like he caught an early standby."

I felt a rush of relief that Myles is here. I looked out the window, "What is that castle like hotel called?"

He came over and stood behind me with his left hand on my shoulder and pointed with his finger against the glass, "That's Excalibur. They have a jousting show you might like."

"I doubt it. I'm more of a dinner show kind of person."

"It is a dinner show. I'll take you if we get a chance. Are you okay?"

"No. I can't seem to focus on one thing at a time. I try, but there's just too much to process at once. My father not being my real father. My real father is a mob enforcer. The man I thought was my father is dead, brutally murdered at that. Then there's being on the run like this, your confusing signals. It's just too much. I need a drink." I laughed.

"Wine okay?"

I turned around. "Wine would be great. It's a little early for Southern Comfort."

"Not here. In Vegas there is no such thing as the wrong time to drink." He went to the kitchen area so I followed.

"I bet it's beautiful here at night with all the lights."

"Yes, but not quite as beautiful as you sweetheart." He pulled the cork free, found two glasses, poured, and handed me one. "Breathe baby."

I exhaled, "How did you know I was holding my breath? I didn't even know."

"I can tell." He took half the wine down in one swig. "Hm, not bad. Bret always did have good taste."

"Bret, he's another brother?"

"Half, yes. He's also a very strange bird. Don't worry, we won't be running into him."

"Good, I've had enough of crazy men lately." I took another sip. "This is very good, buttery, but not too rich. Apricot. Oak barrel. Tastes almost French, but I'm betting it's German."

Lou picked up the bottle and read. "Good Lord, how did you do that?"

"Practice. I took a lot of extra classes in college." I shrugged not wanting to go there right now.

"When you said 'crazy men', does that include me?"

I laughed, "Yes, it most certainly does. In fact, you are the forerunner."

"I am??" He asked like he was surprised.

"Yes. You flirt and call me pet names only boyfriends and husbands should use when talking to a lady. We are *not* a couple, so it leaves me perplexed as to why you would do this." I decided to explore the large rooms and started walking around. More than anything, I don't want him to catch me with those bright blue eyes and say something to knock me off balance again.

"I figure I got your first kiss, I should have the right to call you whatever I want, at least until you find another man." He pushed his hand through his dark brown hair that's just long enough to tie back, if he wanted to.

I closed my eyes. What is he talking about?? Another man? He's not my man!! I opened my eyes and took another sip of wine, this one a little bit larger than a lady should take, but I'm so flustered!

He's sitting on the large red couch sprawled out with is feet on the table. "Can I ask you a personal question?"

I shrugged and went to top off my wine. "Sure."

"Where do you see yourself in five years?"

I laughed, "Probably sitting behind that big desk shuffling papers."

"No, I mean aside from that? Do you want marriage, kids, the white picket fence, all that crap?"

I looked up as Myles came through the door. Saved by the ex-Marine, thank you Myles. I went and hugged him for a long time. "I'm so glad you're here."

He patted my back, "I'm on the clock Miss Whitmore. You can hug me when this is over."

I stepped back. Myles has certain quirks. If he's working, he's very serious and militant. If we're safe somewhere he'll hug me back and make jokes. This is working Myles, my protector, my big brother, and my best friend.

"Okay." I don't apologize because he gets upset if I do. I don't know why. Myles is a bit of a mystery, even to me.

He shook Lou's hand, "Good to see you again friend. Have you been able to contact Paulie?"

"Not yet, but I left word for him to call me. I don't think he's connected me to Miss Whitmore yet. Probably thinks I need a favor, so I'm not surprised he's not replying right away. If you get a hold of him again, drop my name."

"I talked to him on the way up. He thinks I'm the one that took Miss Whitmore out of North Carolina. We have a meeting at sixteen-hundred down in the casino."

"Tonight?? I have to meet him tonight??" I panicked and stepped back.

Lou took my hand, "No honey, just me and Myles for now. We need to know his intentions, read his face for lies, and arrange for the safest meeting we can." He explained.

I nodded, "I wish you didn't have to do this for me."

"It's our job." Myles chimed in then handed Lou a thick manilla envelope. "It's all there."

Lou handed it to me. "I don't want the money. The club will give me the agreed upon cut when I get back. Slider already has the full payment."

"This is for staying on the job, like we discussed." Myles looks confused.

"I said I'd stay on the job, not that I wanted more money. This is personal now. I want to see Miss Whitmore through this, if you still want my help."

"Yes, your help will be valuable, but you should take the money, this could take a while."

"No more money." Lou insisted. "Miss Whitmore is a friend now, I don't take money from friends in need." He clarified and looked at me. "Still think I'm crazy?"

I laughed, "Absolutely."

He shrugged, "Then crazy it is." He held his hand out for Myles to shake. "Shall we get this party started?"

Myles nodded. "Let's do it. I've got four guys downstairs and four out in the hall. There's a car waiting by the front and by the back if we need to get her out of here. I also have keys to the service elevators and all other locked doors. I called her father's pilot Bob, he's on standby with a chopper at a neighboring hotel."

I just felt my jaw drop. How in the world did my mild-mannered ex-marine manage to do all that in what? Hours? I wanted to say something complimentary to the man, but my brain is once again struck dead. What is wrong with me??

Lou's eyebrows went up, "Damn man. You did all that?"

"In the event of Mr. Whitmore's demise I get full control of his resources as long as I'm employed by Miss Whitmore." He looked at me, "I assume I still work for you?"

"Of course!" There's my voice! Good, at least that part of me is still functioning properly.

He looked back at Myles, "Then it's settled. We'll go down at sixteen-hundred, talk to Paulie, and go from there. If Miss Whitmore refuses to meet with Paulie, or he loses his shit, we're out of here immediately." He looked at me, "Put anything you can't live without in your pockets, not a purse. I want you free of baggage if this blows up."

"Okay." I'm feeling a little dizzy so I sat on the big red couch.

"Are you okay honey? You look a little pale." Lou sat next to me taking my hands in his.

I looked into his eyes and felt an instant wash of relief. He's still here. Whew. Everything will be fine. Lou is here, and Myles is here. My protectors. My big strong strapping men. The one holding my hand with the concerned blue eyes is the one I want to lean into right now.

I nodded, "Maybe I should try to eat. Can we go downstairs? I think the chaos will be a good distraction while we wait for six o'clock."

"No." Myles started sweeping the room for bugs. He taught me this years ago one night when we got bored. Myles knows a lot about security, he's taught me a good few things over the years. "You stay in this suite until I give the word. I'll have something brought up if you want."

"Do you think the room is bugged?" I asked. Oh well, so much for a distraction.

"Not by Paulie. The guy who owns this suite on the other hand, would." Myles informed me.

"Someone would bug Bret's room?" I asked.

"Not likely, but he'd bug it to spy on us." Myles replied.

"How do you know my brother?" Lou asked obviously surprised.

"When I got out of the Corps I came here to do some gambling, and other things." He's avoiding telling Lou he was here to have sex with escorts. I already knew this, but maybe he doesn't want Lou to know.

"We met over a poker table down at The Tropicana when it was still a big deal here. Hell, when it was still here. Anyway, I took a shit load of his money, so he put up a company. A security company. It was small, but effective. I won that round too." He plucked a little black thing from a flower pot and examined it. "Dumb-ass, the least you could do is use something that's not in our inventory." He said into the device then dropped it in the ice bucket.

Lou laughed, "Figures Bret would bug his own room, and make sure we knew it was him. I don't know why he cares what we're doing anyway." Lou complained.

Myles kept hunting, "It's just to amuse himself. Bret has a problem, it's called too much money and a whole lot of boredom. If he feels slighted in any way he'll fuck with you just to amuse himself." He looked up at me, "Sorry Miss Whitmore."

I waved it off, "Cuss all you want. At this point I just want this over with." I looked at Lou, "Even if everything is safe, do I still have to meet this Paulie? I don't know if I really want to."

"We'll see. I think you should find out why he's going through all this trouble, and why he killed Mr. Whitmore. Otherwise you'll be left wondering and looking over your shoulder the rest of your life." He explained.

I sighed, "Alright. I'll meet him, if I have to." I know I sound like a whiney little girl, but I can't seem to help it.

Lou ordered a late lunch for the three of us, the extra security guards upstairs, and for the guards downstairs. I thought that was very sweet, until he charged it to the room. Hopefully he'll pay Bret back when this is over.

The guys talked about various scenarios and how they should be handled. I tuned them out to try and organize my own thoughts.

What do I do when this is over? Go home and sit behind that desk again? I'll probably have one hell of a mess to clean up if my father was into making dirty business deals.

My thoughts shifted to what Lou had asked me before Myles got here. Do I want the picket fence? That's a good question. I guess part of me always thought some nice looking young man would cross my path and we'd fall madly in love, have kids . . . . kids. Do I want kids? Not really, at least not now.

Then there's Lou. His hair is too long, but a nice chocolate swirl of colors. I think even if he got a haircut, he should leave the front longer than it should be. I've grown attached to the way he's always shoving it out of his face.

Then there's his long legs and lean waist. I've seen him without a shirt, and minus the tattoos he's quite a piece of work. Something to be drawn with charcoals that capture the shadows his abdominal muscles create.

I'm not sure if I like the tattoos or not. He has such a lovely body, but then again some of the symbols and artwork look important to him. They are all well done, and quite good artistically speaking.

"Barbie!" Lou almost yelled making me jump.

"Shit! Sorry. What?" I looked at him. Did I just cuss? Lou's foul mouth is rubbing off on me. I got a quick flash in my head of Lou's mouth on my neck and shivered. Well that was weird . . . and kind of nice. It left behind a slight adrenaline rush.

"Where were you? I've been trying to get your attention for two minutes." He scolded me.

I felt my mouth twist up, "Nowhere, just thinking." About you. Dammit!! I can't be having thoughts about Lou! He's a drifter, always going from town to town, job to job.

"It's almost six. Myles is going to leave you a couple guns, let's hope you don't need them." He pointed to the table.

I picked up the Glock first and checked the chamber, cartridge, and safety. Then I picked up the .38 to check the bullets. Hollow points, that'll work. "These should help."

Myles stood up. "I'm going to brief the guards outside the door. Lou, I'll see you downstairs."

"You got it." Lou replied then shifted taking both my hands in his. "Look at me baby."

"I can't." I looked out the window.

"Why is that?" He asked softly.

"Because I'll want you to kiss me again before you go." I admitted letting the adrenaline fuel my bravery.

"Is there something wrong with that?" He sounded a little hurt.

I looked at him and saw the humor in his eyes. "Don't tease me Mr. Colson. I have enough on my plate right now."

He sobered, "Very true. How about a quick kiss goodbye then?"

I nodded because I want his lips back on mine so bad it burns in my throat.

He leaned in and touched his lips to mine. I barely got to taste his tongue on mine before he stood letting go of my hands. "Alright kitten, I'll be back as soon as I can."

"Lou?"

He pulled on his cut, "Yes?"

"Thank you, for staying, and helping Myles." Tears stung my eyes.

"I'm not doing this for Myles. Keep the guns close, the volume down on the television so you can hear what's going on in the hallway, and lock the door." He instructed firmly. Gone is the soft Lou, with soft lips, and almost soft beard that tickles my chin. This is the protector. The man on the clock.

I nodded. "Okay. Be careful. Please."

"Always." He turned and left without looking back.

I touched my fingers to my lips. I can still feel his presence here. What am I doing letting this man kiss me?? I must be two biscuits short of a dozen if I'm kissing gypsy bikers with long hair and dazzling blue eyes.

4

The next hour was the longest of my life. When the door opened and the guys walked in I almost ran to them, but I couldn't decide which one to go to first, so I stood up without moving from my spot instead.

"How did it go?" I asked feeling my heart racing.

"Paulie is downstairs waiting for you. We'll be with you the entire time. He has a business proposition for you." Myles didn't sound happy.

"What kind of business proposition?"

"He wouldn't divulge the details, but we agreed on a secure place for us to meet in ten minutes. You should know that if you refuse his offer, he's going to come after you, in every way possible. Business, and personal. He either wants your cooperation, or your life." Myles continued.

I sat back down hard. "He's going to try to kill me tonight?"

"No. We agreed you would have two weeks to bury your . . . Mr. Whitmore, then if you refuse him he'll come after you. I'm sure we can have you well hidden by then." Lou chimed in this time.

"Why the grace period? Why not just take me out here?"

"It's an old custom. Paulie also likes a good game of cat and mouse. He's very angry about whatever went down between himself and your father. I think he wants to see you squirm as he drags out his revenge. He's sick, that's what makes him a good enforcer. When your reputation precedes you people tend to think twice before messing with you and yours." Lou explained rather well. He's pretty good at that. Huh.

"So, if I go along with whatever this is, then he leaves me alone?"

"Yes."

"And if I don't, then I spend the rest of my life running and looking over my shoulder." I determined.

"I'm sure he would give up after a while, but you'd still have to lay low." Myles picked up a kevlar vest. "Put this on just in case."

"I thought you said he wouldn't try to kill me tonight?"

"It's not likely, but I'm not taking any chances. I raised you Barbara. You're the closest thing I have to a daughter. The closest I'll ever have. For the last twenty-three years you're all I've known. I won't lose you to some mob asshole." He informed me simply as he strapped me into the vest.

Lou put one of his own on. "You've been with her since she was born?"

"Yes. From the minute her mother died I've been her parent. Mr. Whitmore dove into his work and left me to see to her care. I changed her diapers and wiped her tears. If anyone is her father, it's me, not him." He replied angrily.

I started crying at his words. Myles doesn't talk like this very often. "I love you too Myles."

He nodded and stepped back, "Alright kid, let's get this over with so I can get some sleep for a change."

"Amen too that." Lou agreed.

"I may never sleep again." I complained as they led me out of the room and down to the casino via the elevator.

We walked to a private gambling room with one poker table, one blackjack table, and a few other tables I didn't recognize. I think that one is a roulette wheel. I know next to nothing about gambling. I can play a mean game of rummy with Myles, but that's about as far as my card playing knowledge goes.

A tall grotesquely round, Italian looking, bald guy in a grey pinstriped Armani suit stood up from one of the tables and looked me over. "Well well, the spitting image of your mother."

"Can we just get this over with?" I asked curtly. I want out of here. This room stinks of scumbags.

He nodded, "Sure, have a seat."

"I'd rather not. I understand you have a business proposition for me?" I want to get to the point so I can go back upstairs and curl up in Lou's arms for what will likely be a good cry, or perhaps a soothing sweet kiss.

"I would appreciate if you would sit." He insisted.

My inner bitch blew on her fingernails and drew up some serious Salem Charm. God bless that school. "I would appreciate it if you would stop telling me what to do, and tell me what you want." Ooh, that sounded good even to me. Now if my heart would stop pounding I might survive this.

He sat back in the chair that looked like it could barely hold the weight of this big fat man. I guess that's where my weight issues come from. "Your mother's looks and my guts. Well, at least you have something going for you. Alright. Have it your way. I want you father's assets. Keep the cash, I want the businesses and all that belongs to them."

"Why?"

"Because he fucked me out of eight million dollars, that's why."

"Fucked you out of, or stole?"

"Is there a difference?" He snapped.

"Yes, if he botched a deal that resulted in you not obtaining said eight million dollars, then the money was never yours to begin with. If the money was yours, and he down right stole it, then I'll see that you get the money back, plus interest if you would be so kind as to agree to stay out of my life." I can hear the venom in my tone and it's giving me another adrenaline rush. This one is a burning rush that reminds me of the rush I get shooting. It's very empowering.

He looked impressed. "It was a botched deal, one I had invested a lot of time procuring."

"That, Mr. Marconni, is the price of doing business. Sometimes you win, sometimes you lose. Unless you can provide some kind proof that my father took money from you, this discussion is over. I will retain my father's assets, and his cash. Will there be anything else this evening Mr. Marconni?" I tried to sound like a bored waitress.

"You have two weeks to bury your father. Then I'm coming after you so hard and fast you won't know what hit you."

"I'm afraid you'll have to catch me first. Good day to you sir." I turned and started for the door.

"Oh, Miss Whitmore? One more thing."

I turned back, "Yes?"

"If you're going to do this, I'm going to expose you to the mob as my child."

I thought for a second, "Well then, this shall be a most entertaining dual Mr. Marconni. I look forward to the challenge, and to the day where I bury the sperm donor who was so kind as to donate to my DNA. I'm afraid we're both going to discover just how much we are, and are *not* alike. Good evening sir."

I turned and walked through the doors and straight for the bar. The guys are on my heels, but I can't look at them yet.

The bartender came over wide-eyed seeing all the bullet-proof vests flanking me. He probably thinks I'm famous, or rich, I don't have the looks of a celebrity. "What can I get you Miss?"

"Double SoCo, rocks, and get my friends here whatever they want, on me." I almost smiled at the look on his face, but I'm still shaking from that encounter.

Was that really me in there? I was scared out of my mind until I stood my ground. Then the adrenaline and Salem Charm kicked in. Wow that was quite a rush!.

I took my drink and two sips before looking at Myles, "How'd I do?"

His eyebrows went up, "You have to ask? You were fucking amazing."

Lou put his hand on my shoulder so I looked at him now, "You were incredible. Who was that woman in there? I about fell out of my boots when you told him off the way you did. Talk about an ice queen. Remind me not to piss you off." He shook his head and placed his order with the bartender for a beer.

I took another soothing sip then said, "I don't know about all that, he scared the begeezus out of me."

They both laughed as the bartender continued to hand out drinks.

I sat on a stool now that my legs have discovered they can't function without the surge of adrenaline running through them. "Oh man. That was a rush!" I laughed.

"You're telling me." Lou complained. "I thought you were going to goad him into a gunfight right then and there."

"He wants that money too bad. I'll die before I give that bastard a dime." I promised.

Lou lifted my chin, "You realize you can't go home. That's where he's going to look for you first."

"I know. I'll figure something out."

"We can have Mr. Whitmore cremated and his ashes sent here if you want." Myles suggested.

I shrugged, "Do whatever you want. I'll pay for the services and funeral, but I have no desire to go, or to have his ashes here. Put him on the mantel at home, or in the ground, makes no difference to me."

"Maybe you should think about it for a day or two." Lou suggested.

"Maybe I was lied to my entire life and now I'm left picking up his dirty laundry. He's never been there for me, why would I be there for him?"

"Just think about it." Lou encouraged.

I looked at him, "If you're going to second guess every move I make, you can leave now. Besides, the job is over. Myles can take it from here." I assured him.

Lou's eyes suddenly filled with anger. "Are you asking me to leave?"

"No, I'm telling you if you're going to second guess my every move, then yes, you may leave."

"I think we should have a little talk." He decided. "Privately."

"I'm done talking tonight." I stepped around him and headed for the elevators. I don't know why I'm suddenly lashing out at Lou. I need to be alone to think. This whole mess just got real serious, and I feel like I'm in way over my head suddenly. I can't believe I just challenged a mob boss. Somehow I've lost my marbles in the last week.

Myles pulled Lou aside while we waited for the doors to open. "Dude, let it go for now."

Lou nodded, "Alright." He sighed, "For now."

"Thank you." Myles smacked Lou on the shoulder and walked back to me. "Want to get drunk and watch stupid television shows we hate?" We like to mock the bad acting in old television shows. I secretly love the shows, maybe Myles does too. It's a mystery I'd rather not solve to be honest.

I laughed, "Yes, desperately."

"Right this way." He held the door open for me.

Lou remained outside the elevator doors looking in at Myles. "I'm going to go out for a bit, give her some space."

I looked at him, "You don't . . ."

"Yes. I do. I'll see you in a bit." He turned and left disappearing into the casino.

"Shit." I looked up at Myles. "I messed that up pretty bad didn't I?"

"No. He's madly in love with you Barbara. Can't you tell?"

"What?? He is not!!!"

"Sorry kid, but that poor guy is head over heels for you. I called him out on it on the way back from the first meeting. I don't think he realized it until then, kind of fucked with his head."

"Oh no." I covered my face. "I am such an idiot. I just told him to leave."

"He's not leaving. It would take a lot more than some snippy comment from you to run him off."

"Where did he go?"

"Not a clue, but if I was him, I'd be halfway to a good drunk by now."

I laughed, "Oh God. This should be interesting later. He better not puke on Bret's pretty floors."

"Don't worry about that, it would serve Bret right, the guy really is an ass." He assured me with a hint of humor in his voice.

I laughed. "Poor Lou. I feel like I should go find him."

"I think maybe he could use some time alone to sort out his own feelings." The doors opened so he looked out first getting the nod from the guard by the door to continue. "What about your feelings? Do you like Mr. Colson?"

"I like him just fine, now." I added remembering our rather bumpy start. "I can't love him, it would never work. Besides, we barely know each other." I went to get a bottle of wine, corkscrew, and a glass to take to the couch.

"You never know, you could be made for each other." He teased grabbing a beer and joining me on the couch.

I laughed, "No, we are certainly not made for each other. Look at my life, look at his. It would never work. He'd be bored with me in a week anyway."

"I seriously doubt that. And your lives aren't so different anymore. If you think you're going to be able to just sit still and shuffle papers at your desk all day you're wrong. Paulie is going to chase you down until he gets what he wants. You're going to have to stay on the run, unless you want to hand over eight million dollars."

I groaned and downed the first glass. "I hate it when you're right. But still, he doesn't have to run with me. He's got his job, I have my drama . . . it's too much. I doubt we'd be able to stay on the move together. I don't even know what I've gotten myself into yet."

"I can have everything about the company brought to you. You can work from just about anywhere these days with all the latest technology and internet popping up everywhere."

"I know." I reached over and picked up the remote. "It's not just that. He's a big bad biker. I'm a Barbie, as he calls me."

Myles laughed, "I'm surprised you let him get away with calling you that."

"He calls me all kinds of things I wish he wouldn't." I complained over my wine.

"Like what?"

"It doesn't matter. The pet names don't bother me as much as being used as a body pillow every night."

Myles choked on his beer, "WHAT??"

I waved him off, "It's not like that. He doesn't touch me. He said he does it so he can protect me better, and I always fall asleep with my back to him, but somehow he ends up draped all over me in the morning. In the RV I understood, the bed was small, but in a king size bed you'd think he'd find enough room of his own not to smother me."

Just then Lou opened the door and Myles stood up. Lou looked at Myles, then at me. "Is something wrong?"

Myles stepped around the table before I could catch up and figure out what he was doing. "I'll say there's something wrong."

I jumped up and ran to get in Myles' face. "Wait, it's not like that. He's never touched me, I swear."

He looked down at me. "Are you sure? Because I can rip him apart right here."

"I'm sure. I'd tell you if I wasn't sure, you know that." I reminded him.

He nodded, "Alright. I'm going down to gamble a months salary away." He looked at Lou, "Keep your hands to yourself."

Lou lifted an eyebrow at him before turning it on me, "Would you mind telling me what that was all about?"

"I made the mistake of complaining about you using me as you human body pillow. He took it wrong. I said it wrong. Whatever." I threw my hand up in the air and went back to the sofa. I give up.

Lou sat down beside me after shedding his leather and kevlar. "He's right though. I overstepped the boundaries."

"Yes, you did." I agreed.

"I'm sorry. I don't know what gets into me, except I have this need to be close to you. To hold you. That, and you smell really good."

"I smell like cheap hotel body wash." I argued.

"Not that smell, your smell. Everyone has a distinct scent, one all their own. Yours is intoxicating."

"There you go, saying all these sweet things again, muddling my brain." I topped off my wine and sat back to look at the television.

"Maybe tonight isn't the night for this kind talk." He decided and sat back too.

"What kind of talk?"

"The talk where I tell you I love you and you're stuck with me." He said so simply it took me a second.

"You can't possibly love me Lou, you barely know me. besides, you hate everything about me. My snobby way of talking. My fancy spoiled rich bitch clothes. About the only nice thing you've said about my appearance, involved curves I am none too proud of."

He exhaled in frustration and scratched the back of his head. "Boy, you are on fire tonight."

"I'm just pointing out the truth. I've grown to like you, maybe you've grown to like me a little, but that's all it is.

Not only that, but my life is about to go into a tailspin. I have no idea what I'm in for with Paulie and my father's companies."

"I have a pretty good idea what you're in for, which is why I'm not leaving you alone to deal with it."

"I have Myles." I argued.

"Myles is a body guard, he specializes in security, a lot like myself, but he can't help you sort out the business."

"And you can?"

"Maybe I can, maybe I can't, but I know who can." He assured me.

"Maybe you were right. We should discuss this another time."

"Excellent." He reached for my wine glass, downed it, and set it on the table. Then he scooped me up like a bride. "I have a better idea anyway."

"What exactly do you have in mind?"

He tossed me on the large bed then turned back to close the doors.

I scrambled back on the bed. "Lou?"

He pulled his shirt off and tossed it on the chair. Then he leaned over and grabbed my foot dragging me to him. I fell on my back as he crawled over me.

I put my hands on his shoulders and looked into his eyes. There's a burning need in those eyes I've never seen before. "This can't be a good idea."

"Oh, it's a very good idea." He teased me by nipping along my jaw. "A very good idea."

"What are you going to do?"

He touched his lips to mine suddenly. "I'm going to kiss you until you agree to marry me." His mouth crushed mine halting the 'What??' I was about to scream.

Damn him. This man has my number, and all he's doing is kissing me! Oh, he's so yummy. Ah screw it. I wrapped my arms around his neck and found his hair to be very soft between my fingers. Now this is the kind of distraction I can sink my teeth into.

I wallowed in his kiss because this is so much better than the last week of my life. He's making everything go away and replacing it with himself. His loving eager kisses that are leaving me breathless and aching in places I've never ached before.

I pushed on his chest so he lifted up. "Wait. I can't breathe."

He smiled and moved my hair off my face. "You are even more beautiful when you're flushed and panting."

"I think we should stop."

He looked playfully confused, "Oh really? Why is that?"

"You know why." I tried to sit up but he didn't budge so I laid back down. "Lou, don't."

"Is there a problem?"

"Yes!! I don't know what to do . . . with . . . this." I pointed to him and then to myself and back again.

"Ah. It has nothing to do with that ache between your legs?"

I covered my face. "How can you know that??"

"Easy, I have the same ache." He took my hand away. "I can take it away, without taking your virtue. Just a touch, and I can make you sleep like a baby."

Oh God that sounds really good. "I . . . don't know."

"Okay, tell you what. When you want me to stop, just say stop. I won't do anything you don't want me to." He promised.

"What are you going to do?"

He rolled off to his side and flipped the top button of my jeans open. "Just touch." He slid the zipper down and that ache came back ten fold.

"Barbara, look at me." He insisted softly.

"I'm so nervous." I lifted my knees and leaned them to my left.

"That's okay, just try to relax a little. Put your legs down." He slid down, took my boots off, and then grabbed my jeans pulling them completely off. He climbed back on the bed between my legs and lowered his head. Then he inhaled right on the top of my panties!! "You smell as sweet as you look."

"Oh my God!!" I don't know whether to beg for more or try to run.

He laughed and slid up alongside me. He looked down into my eyes. "Keep your eyes open. I want to see you."

"What do I do?" I asked nervously.

"Nothing. Have you ever, you know, taken care of things yourself?"

"What things?"

He closed his eyes, "You have *got* to be kidding me."

"What??" Is he disappointed?

He looked at me again with some kind of primal need. "I'm going to touch you now."

I nodded. "Does it hurt?"

"No, not just touching. When I take your virginity it will hurt a little, but we're a ways from that. Just enjoy yourself." He took that wandering hand of his and ran his fingers just under my panty line. "I think we'll make this one quick."

He slid his hand over my mound pushing my legs apart. He held his hand firmly over me and something jumped inside me.

Then he brought his hand back like he was going to leave me, but he stopped. I don't know what he did, but suddenly he's rubbing me and the anxiety in my belly exploded into a million pieces radiating to every limb and caressing it gloriously.

"Oh sweet Geezus." Lou's fingers found me wet, very wet. "Oh baby, let's see if we can get another one of those for ya." He started again and the explosion slammed into me so hard I screamed and grabbed the bedsheets to keep from floating off into space.

I felt him slow and move his hand lower. His finger gently probed without entering me. The pumping continued and I felt that need for release building again. How many times can a person do this??

Turns out four is my limit. "Okay, you win!"

He laughed and set me free of his glorious torment. "I love you Barbara Whitmore, more than you will ever know."

I looked up at him as he kissed my forehead and rolled off the bed. "Where are you going?"

He lifted the covers. "Roll over here. I'm going to take a cold shower. You get some sleep."

"A cold shower? Why would you do that?" I slid over so he could tuck me in between the sheets.

"Because I'm a gentleman Miss Whitmore, and you've had enough for one day."

"Oh." It suddenly hit me why men take cold showers. "Sorry."

He kissed my forehead and both cheeks, when I tried for a real kiss he shook his finger at me, "No more for you tonight. I'm a man, not a saint." He tapped my nose. "Sleep baby."

I closed my eyes and thought back to the wonderful things he'd just made me feel. Well, now I get what all the fuss is about! The thought made me smile as I fell blissfully into a dreamless sleep.

5

When I woke up Lou was once again draped all over me. This time I laid still and touched his hair. "What am I to do with you?" I whispered as low as I could.

He groaned, "I told you, marry me." He replied softly.

"I am in no condition to marry anyone. What brought all this on anyway?"

He kept his head on my chest and nuzzled me with his nose. This is the closest he's gotten to my breasts since we've been 'sleeping' together. I should be bothered, but I'm too comfortable.

"I think it was a gradual process. The more I touch you, and kiss you, the more I want. I like just sitting in the same room with you too, watching the way you move so gracefully, it's like you're made of water."

"Well, the human body is 80 percent water." I tugged his hair, "I need to use the restroom."

He lifted up and looked down at me, "Will you come back?"

"I think that would be a bad idea right now. I need to figure things out Lou."

"About us? Or about your father?"

"I think both."

He took a deep breath and let it out slowly. "Alright, but just so you know, I'm not going to be so easy for you to toss aside. I see how you look at me. You have to see what you're doing to me. I'll make you my bride if it's the last thing I do." He warned me.

"What makes you so sure you want me?" I asked as he sat upright to let me out from under him.

"Everything. Your smile, your hips, your quick wit, and smart, but always polite, mouth. The way you handled Big Paulie about gave me a stiffy on the spot." He laughed and fell on his back. "And then the way you smell, and last night. Geezus kitten, you have so much passion it's impossible to stop thinking about."

"I think you might be nuts. Where are my pants?" I looked around on the floor.

He pointed to the other side of the bed, "Over there somewhere."

"Will you kindly retrieve them for me?"

He looked at me, "I've already seen you in your skivvies. You don't need to be shy around your future husband."

"Lou . . . please." I begged. "I have no sense of humor before coffee."

"Nah. You want 'em, you get 'em." He's enjoying my torment.

I grabbed the blanket and pulled, but he's laying on it. I slept under the covers, he slept on top, as usual. "Now look."

He's laughing.

I grabbed a pillow and smacked him in the face, "Go get my pants!!"

He's laughing harder now as he steals the pillow and tosses it to the floor.

"Lou!!" Now I'm laughing despite my frustration at this suddenly childish man.

He reached out and started pulling the blanket slowly away from me. "Are you shy little kitten?"

"Yes!!" He looks so playful and sweet I can't help but feel like a kid myself.

He finished pulling the blanket away and then the sheet. Then it turned into a wrestling match that was quite fun! I've never wrestled with anyone except Myles, and that was self-defense training, not play. Nothing like this. He tickled my sides and put exaggerated kisses all over my neck making me squirm. If it wasn't so much fun I might be humiliated.

He finally let me up even though he pretended to chase me to the bathroom. I was still laughing and smiling like an idiot when I shut the door and leaned my back against it. He really does know how to distract a girl. I'm sure he's had plenty of practice. A pang of jealously hit me. I pushed it away refusing to let it ruin my giddy mood. I'm not sure I've ever been giddy before. Thank you Lou.

Over breakfast I decided to brave a question that's been nagging at me since this morning when he said I have so much passion. "I have a, strange question."

"Ask me anything you want kitten." He said cutting into his pancakes.

"Is it . . . like that, for everyone?"

He looked up, "What?"

"What you did to me in there, last night." I pointed to the bedroom. "Is it like that for everyone?"

He smiled big and wicked, "No baby. Not that I know of."

"Then . . . I'm so confused." I laughed at myself.

"Sex feels good to most, great to some, and from what I understand, fantastic to the few who find that connection like I found with you. When we make love, we're really gonna lose our minds." He promised and bit the pancakes off his fork quickly, playfully, with promises in his eyes. Wicked, sultry eyes.

I blushed, "You make it sound like it's been decided."

"In my book, it is decided. I'm not going to let you go Barbara. You will be mine, and I'm going to enjoy every second it takes to seduce you."

"I get butterflies in my stomach when you talk like that." I said as my face heated up.

"Tell me something. When you told me I could leave last night, down in the casino, would you have let me walk out that door never to be seen again?"

I felt my heart clench around my stomach. "I . . ." The idea of not waking up with him laying all over me hit me hard. Right in the chest. "My pride would have let you, but I would have regretted it."

"That's what I needed to hear. I'm not going anywhere baby. You need me, and I need you."

"What about your job?"

He shrugged, "I can afford some time off. When things settle down for you I'll pick up a few jobs to pay the bills. Right now I have plenty of money in the bank for us to live on until then."

"No, I . . . I didn't mean the money. I have more money than sense. I thought you liked it. I don't want to take over your life." I can't figure out what I'm trying to say.

"The work is fine, but it's not everything. You on the other hand, are everything. Don't worry about me, or money. Your assets might get seized when this shit hits the fan anyway. I don't want your money Barbara, I hope you know that." He looked at me with scolding and daring eyes.

"Yes, I know that. My life is about to do a somersault. I could be neck deep in my father's illegal activities. This could be an awful mess to sort out, and in two weeks Paulie is going to start coming after me. I'll be running for my life and trying to fight for what's mine. Mr.

Whitmore may not have been my biological father, but the people working for him are now my responsibility. If I can't handle it, I have to see that it's sold off to anyone but Paulie."

"You've given this a good deal of thought."

"A little. I want to make sure you really want to get involved in this mess. I also don't want to fall any further in love with you only to have you leave in a few months, or ask for a divorce because it's too much." I finally said it! The marriage part was a little over the top as far as I was concerned, but he kept bringing it up.

"Ah. So you think so little of me that I would just up and leave you because shit got a little tough. Honey, I *live* tough, it's nothing new to me. My experience as a Transporter will serve to keep you from having to look over your shoulder all the time. I'll keep you safe, and you can concentrate on how to protect your new empire. I want to be with you, even just sitting here eating breakfast, and talking. This is all I need." He smiled, "Now my wants are a little different story." He flirted with a look before continuing, "All you need to know about how I feel is that I love you. And when you're ready I'm going to put you in front of a priest and marry you. Then I'm going to spend the rest of my life riding you when I'm not riding my Harley." He teased with a playful smile.

I put my hand to my stomach. "Oh my. You *really* can't say things like that."

He laughed, "It's a biker thing. When some of us get married they throw in the vow to ride the old lady as much as the bike. I don't know where it started, but most us get a good laugh when somebody uses it."

"It's . . . kind of sexy, but weird." I laughed at myself and my ignorance of his world. Which brought my head up and my fork down. "Speaking of which. How do I fit into your world. I mean, I wear dresses, not jeans and leather."

He sat back looking like a big playful man with a secret.

"What??"

"I just pictured you in a short leather skirt sitting on my bike. I might need another cold shower."

I put my hands over my face. "Oh my God! I would never have the guts to wear something like that."

"I bet you would. Finish your breakfast. We'll go take care of an errand with the Vegas chapter, then I'll take you shopping. Vegas is the perfect city for shopping."

Myles walked through the door, "Hey kid, you okay?"

I blinked a couple times. "Yeah, I'm just . . . yes, I'm fine." I laughed.

Lou spoke up, "Hey buddy, we cool?"

"Is she okay?" Myles pointed to me.

"Ask her. We're just having a bit of fun over breakfast. You walked in after I said something that made her blush." He explained for me.

I looked up at Myles and smirked, "That's true. Do all men have such silver tongues with women?"

"I wouldn't know." Myles went to fix himself a plate.

I listened as Lou asked him, "No wife or girlfriend?"

"No. I got my first love killed right after high school. Then I went into the Marines for a four year tour. Mr. Whitmore hired me right away when my duty was up. He said he wanted somebody he could trust and promised me a job for life, and a killer retirement package if I took care of his daughter." He sat with a giant plateful of eggs pancakes and bacon and dove in.

"You haven't had a girlfriend the entire time?" Lou asked putting his hands on my shoulders as he stood behind me now.

Myles shook his head and looked at Lou with some kind of warning look.

"Ah. Well buddy, I plan to marry this young lady right here, so maybe now you can have a little free time to find one."

Myles swallowed, "Don't want one. There was only one for me, she's dead. Change the subject." He looks mad.

"Yes, change the subject." I stood up, "Is Myles going with us today?"

"If he wants to." Lou replied.

"Where are you going?" Myles asked.

"I need to go pick up some money for a job I did last month, then I was going to take my girl here shopping, then hopefully on a real date later tonight." Lou explained. "You're welcome to come meet the Vegas chapter, but the rest could be right boring."

"I'll go because I'm still not convinced Paulie will keep to his word about the two weeks. I've been shopping with Miss Whitmore her entire life, I think I'll live."

Lou laughed, "Maybe, until you see what I want to buy her."

I looked at Lou, "Don't do that."

"What did I do??" He put his hands up in the air and stepped back with a smile.

I felt my eyes roll, "I cooked, you can clean."

"Housekeeping will take care of it." He informed me.

"I keep looking for my purse." I looked around not knowing what to do with myself. These two are making me very uncomfortable.

"What's wrong Barbara?" Myles asked noticing my inability to stand still.

"I need to get out of this room!!"

Those idiots both laughed at me, so I left taking one of the bodyguards outside the door with me down to the casino. Good thing I stuck some cash in my back pocket from the envelope Myles had tried to give to Lou yesterday.

I walked around the casino for a few minutes before I sat down at a Black Jack table and asked the dealer for the basic rules.

He explained them as clearly as if he'd done it a thousand times. He probably has. The concept seems simple enough. More than anything I just want a distraction. I put two hundred dollars on the table in exchange for chips right about the time my two idiots joined me. My idiots. I love my idiots, and therefore I'm the only one allowed to call them that, and I would only do it in my head, never out loud. Neither of them is really an idiot.

"It's like having giant shadows." I complained trying to fight a smile as the dealer dealt the first hand.

"Do me a favor, don't walk out like that again." Lou said as he leaned into my ear.

"She knows better." Myles added. "Right?" He shot me a dirty look as he sat on my other side pushing some guy down a seat. Normally I would scold him, but I'm in no mood to play mother hen with either of these two men at the moment.

"Stop yelling at me. It's been a rough week." I tapped the table for another card and counted to twenty two. Rats.

"If I was yelling my dear, the entire casino would know it." Myles scolded me. He hates it when I do things like this. I try not to make his life difficult, but sometimes a girl just needs to get out of the room.

I looked up and almost fell out of my chair when Paulie sat down. "I wondered if you would risk leaving your room. I see you're as much the whore your mother was." He looked at Myles and then Lou.

Both men started to stand. I put my hand on their arms to reign them in. "No fighting gentlemen. What I do, or do not do, is of no concern to you Mr. Marconni."

"Just an observation." He slid money across the table for chips and the next round began. How befitting. This feels like round two with this sweaty pig of a man. I can't believe I carry his DNA. I shuttered at the thought before replying, "An observation based on your inability to do your homework. You know what they say about assumptions." Oh, I'm in *just* the right mood for this. I welcome verbal warfare at this point. Instead of snapping at Lou I can snap at the reason I'm snippy to begin with.

"That's quite a mouth you have there, daughter." He let the last word slither out like the snake he is.

"It comes with a brain, something you would no nothing about."

Lou coughed. "Easy babe."

"Stay out of this." I snapped. "Hit me." I told the dealer. Twenty-one, score.

"You know Miss Whitmore, you might be interested to know you have three brothers and a sister." Paulie told me.

"I have what's left of my family sitting on either side of me thank you very much. Sharing the same blood does not mean we are 'family', it means we're biologically related. Rest assured it ends there for me Mr. Marconni."

"That's too bad, they were looking forward to introducing themselves." He waved his hand in the air, "Maybe another time then."

"What do you want Mr. Marconni?" Myles asked.

I put my hand on his arm, "We already know what he wants, please don't engage. I can handle myself just fine."

Lou sat back a little like he'd just discovered the best show on earth. Wise man kept his mouth shut.

"So, you like bossing grown men around?" Paulie went right back to it. He's trying to provoke me, or the guys. Maybe both.

I will not be provoked. "I take no pleasure in 'bossing' anyone around." I said simply taking a loss to the dealer even with a nineteen. This game is almost as frustrating as the pig a couple seats away.

"You could save yourself a lot of hassle and heartache by just giving me what's mine." He took a twenty-one and I wanted to throw my drink at him. Lou had ordered me a glass of wine when he first sat down.

"If I remember correctly, you never had possession of the said eight million dollars. Not to mention there is no evidence that my father caused you to lose the business deal in question. If you want to come after me, Mr. Marconni, you're going to have to do a lot better than that." I looked up at him feeling my inner bitch slip right into my seat.

He stared back at me, "You're going to regret going up against me."

"I'm not the one going up against you, you're the one who is going up against me. I don't feel the need to make threats and warn you with promises of pain, suffering, and eminent death as you do. The results of your audacity will reveal themselves all in good time." I assured him.

He ran his fat finger over his fat jaw. "Maybe I should have hired you instead of making you an enemy."

"You cannot afford me sir." I informed him.

His eyes are darting a little now. "I believe you will be the first worthy opponent I've had in years."

"Then maybe you should start choosing your battles more wisely. There is no honor is wiping out the weak. However, when you take down the king in his own castle, that's a victory worth celebrating." I took my losses and stood up. "I plan to do a lot of celebrating at your expense Mr. Marconni." I started to leave then turned back almost bumping into Lou.

"By the way Mr. Marconni, be careful how you judge a book by it's cover." I waved my hand over my body. "You might think you're getting this, but in fact, you're getting these." I thumbed both thumbs at the two very large men who are dead set on protecting me. "And these, are not to be taken lightly, neither are their associates." I gave him a second to reply. When he didn't I turned and left straight for the main entrance. I need air.

Once outside I looked up at Myles, "Did you bring them?"

He gave me a look but reached into his inside pocket for my clove cigarettes. I don't really smoke, but I like a good clove now and then, just like a man likes a good cigar.

"You smoke?" Lou asked.

I lit the stogie and inhaled. "Not all the time, just when I'm having a moment."

Lou took my chin in his hand, "You have no idea how much I love you. I've never seen a woman, or a man, talk so goddamned elegantly and at the same time to put a person in their place. Once again, that was beautiful baby."

I shrugged. "He's an idiot."

"No, Paulie is one of the most difficult men to beat in the business. He's not stupid, he's greedy, which makes him dangerous." He kissed my forehead and let go so I could smoke.

"Greed bleeds stupid Mr. Colson." I argued then immediately felt like a shit, "I'm sorry. I'm still in bitch mode here."

He smiled, "It's okay, your bitch mode is right sexy."

I rolled my eyes.

"Geeze. Maybe I will skip the shopping spree. You got this Lou?" Myles asked.

"I'm armed and ready. I'll keep Max around for extra eyes."

"Thanks. I'm going to go for a ride before returning the bike this afternoon. That alright?"

"You bet. Ride safe."

Myles waved from over his shoulder as he left.

"Is he mad?" Lou asked me.

"No. You're taking over his job, it's messing with his head. Myles is a complicated guy, don't worry, he'll be fine. He just needs another full-time client. Maybe I can find him one."

"I think I have a better idea."

"Oh yeah?" I looked up and into his bright blue eyes for the first time since we left the breakfast table this morning.

"I'll talk to him about it later. Come on, you can finish your smoke while we walk around to get my bike."

"It's funny, yesterday that thing scared the daylights out of me. Today I can't wait to get back on it with you." I laughed as we walked.

"She."

"What?" I looked up as he put my arm around his waist. "She. Cars, boats, and motorcycles are all she's, not it's."

"I've heard that before. Why is that?"

"Because there are only two things that can bring a man to his knees, his old lady he loves, and the bike he covets."

"How do they bring you to your knees?"

"When I propose to you, it will be on my knees. When I work on my bike, I'm usually on my knees, or a brake cart, but either way, you get my point."

"Am I going to be the other woman, fighting for your affection against a motorcycle?" I teased.

"No. You my dear, will never need to fight for my affection. I can get a new bike, you are not replaceable."

"Aww." I hugged him as I leaned into him. "Maybe I should marry the silver-tongued devil after all."

"Maybe you should." He agreed as we reached his bike.

I took the helmet and jacket he handed me from his saddle bags. "Thanks. Why don't you wear a helmet?"

"Because I need to be able to see. Helmets get in the way."

"What if you crash?"

"I've dropped a bike a time or two in my day. Both times I was wearing a helmet and couldn't see in my peripheral vision. Almost got shot the second time. That's when I hung the helmet up. I haven't had an incident since." He explained.

"I'm glad you're okay, but do me a favor, go slow for me today. I'm still a bundle of nerves after that Black Jack game."

"No problem, we're not going far." He swung his leg over and righted the large machine. Then he held his hand out, "Ready?"

"Definitely." I took his hand and thankfully managed to climb on without tripping over myself this time.

6

Meeting the Las Vegas chapter was not unlike meeting the Exiles. The men were rough and tough looking, but greeted us like long lost friends. Lou introduced me as his old lady, earning a few looks of surprise.

We spent about an hour socializing before he rode us back to the main part of town. I'm starting to feel a little more comfortable around all these bikers. It helps that Lou is right by my side the whole time.

He took us back to the hotel and parked near where we were before. Questions had built up in my mind along the ride about his life, and his family.

He helped me off the bike so I don't trip and burn myself on the hot pipes. Then he kissed me so suddenly, and so passionately I dropped my helmet. Whoa! What's this?? What did I do?? How do I do it again???

When he let me up for air I asked, "What was that for?"

"You. Last night, this morning in the casino, and the way you clung to me at the club. I was the envy of every man in your path today." He tucked my helmet and jacket in the saddle bags.

"I don't see how. Did you see all those super-models at that club? I felt like a fat cow in comparison." I complained.

He grabbed my arm, "Come here."

"What?"

He looked at me then his bike and back again. "Here, just play along." He scooped me up and positioned my legs and arms in some silly pose. He did something with my hair. The way he's looking me over is making me feel self conscious.

"I feel silly."

"You won't in a minute." He stepped back and took about six pictures with his phone from different angles.

I hopped off having had enough of this type of attention. "Okay enough, you're embarrassing me."

He tapped the screen on his phone and showed it to me. "Look. This is what I see when I look at you."

I cringed but looked anyway. "That's not me. That's . . . holy moly, is that really . . . me? I flipped through the pictures. "What the hell??"

He laughed snatching his phone back. "That one's going on my wallpaper."

"You better not!" I still can't believe that was me. The woman displayed in such an erotic fashion on that big beautiful bike could *not* have been me. I'm not sexy!!

"Oh yes, you can bet your beautiful ass that's going on my wallpaper." He threatened taking me under his arm again, "Ready to go see how beautiful you really are?"

"No. Yes. I don't know!" The idea of playing sex goddess for the day is kind of exciting, but mostly scary. I don't wear short skirts, hell, I don't even like to show cleavage.

"Do you trust me?" He asked probably sensing my apprehension.

"That's a strange question to ask."

"I need to know Barbara." He scolded playfully.

"I guess I do. I mean, yes, I believe I trust you almost as much as I trust Myles, which is more than I trust anyone."

"We'll have to work on that. I want you to trust me as much, if not more. I will be your husband, you should be able to trust your husband."

"Oh my God, can we curb the marriage talk for today??"

"Nope. I am relentless, and you will succumb to my charms." He decided as we stepped out into the sun.

"I believe I already did, last night." I flirted reminding him.

He groaned, stopped, turned and cupped my face quickly before kissing me good. I forgot where we were as he made love to my mouth with his.

When somebody hooted at us he grabbed my hair and gently tilted my head back. His eyes are burning with that need I remember from our time in the bedroom.

There are about ten people standing around. Every woman is looking at Lou like they want to jump him right here in the street. The men are looking at me. I have no idea why. He's the one doing the passionate kissing in the middle of the street!

I buried my face in his chest. "I can't believe you just did that."

"Oh honey, the things I'm going to do to you . . . that will seem like nothing." He promised.

"Like what??" I'm horrified. Can it get anymore . . . public display of affection?

"You'll see. I'm going to slowly peel away these inhibitions of yours, starting today."

"I'm scared." I laughed.

"Good, makes for better sex." He teased kissing the top of my head.

"It does??"

"Not real fear, like fear of your life, or fear of getting hurt. However, the fear of getting caught can be quite erotic."

"Caught? Where are people having sex? In the streets??"

He laughed and pointed to a side street. "Right down there about two blocks is an empty warehouse. I know for a fact it's unlocked because I broke the lock chasing some asshole a few months ago. The building is set for destruction, but they don't have the proper permits in order yet. I could easily put your back to the wall and your legs around my waist. Hmm. Damn I need I drink, a very strong, and very cold drink." He pulled me into another casino.

"Would you really do that?" I asked as we waited for our drinks.

He ran his thumb over my cheek. "Yes, in a heartbeat."

"But . . .

"Stop thinking about it, and especially stop talking about it. Or baby, I'm going to throw you down and kiss your clothes off right here and now."

I swallowed turning bright red as the lady behind us gasped. I took my Jack and Coke from the bartender and tried to thank him but the words wouldn't come out. Hopefully the forced smile was enough.

"Now. Let's go find some clothes that fit your perfect little curves." He once again draped his arm around my shoulders and just like that escorted me back outside.

"Did you hear that girl? She gasped at what you said." I laughed taking a sip. "Are we allowed to drink outside?"

"They're plastic cups, so yes. Cops don't care too much, they won't bother you with plastic, but glass and drunks don't mix."

I laughed, "Where are we going?"

"Caesar's Palace baby. That's where the good stuff is."

I turned in front of the mirror. I can't wear this!! It's cut clear up to my tush. The boots come up to just over my knee. And these stockings?? And where did I get such huge boobs?? I knew they weren't small, but in this dress they look huge!

I looked at my rear end one more time in the mirror. "Lou is going to run for the hills." I laughed at myself and figured better he run now than later.

I opened the door and peeked out finding him waiting with his arms crossed just outside the door. "Is there anyone around?" I asked. His pose reminds me of Flagstaff when he kissed me in the dressing room. That seems so long ago now for some reason.

"Just hold the door open and step back." He said in a husky voice I don't think I've heard before.

I stepped back holding the door open and did a little 'ta-da!' with my hands feeling absolutely ridiculous.

He looked me over. "Turn around, slowly."

I did and screamed when he was on me and kicking the door shut. He cupped my face and looked into my eyes. I thought he was going to kiss me, but instead he took my shoulders and turned me to face the mirror.

I had to blink to focus. "Well, with you in the reflection I don't feel so big." Lou is a big man who dwarfs just about everyone, except Myles. He and Myles are built differently, but they are about he same height and girth.

"You are not big." He brought his hands around and under my breasts. "Okay, these are big."

I laughed, "I know! I had no idea! I feel so slutty!!"

"Yeah, I think we'll buy this one for the bedroom." He bent down and kissed my neck. "I have something else I want you to try on that you can wear in public."

Relief washed over me. "Thank God, I thought you were going to make me wear this out there!" I pointed to the front of the store.

He smiled, "No, I want to keep some things to myself." He opened the door and reached out for a handful of hangers with clothes hanging from them. "See what you can do with these."

I took the hangers and put them on the hooks.

"Ah hell." He closed the door again and backed me to the mirror. His fingers came up and tickled along the swells under my breasts. "May I?"

I nodded because I can't breathe let alone talk. What's he going to do?

He moved the material aside and lowered to take one in each hand before closing his mouth over my left nipple. When he suckled I made a whimpering type noise I've never heard from myself before.

"Oh my." I felt my head fall back against the mirror as I gripped his shoulders for balance.

He groaned before finding the other nipple and suckled a little harder as he kneaded the tender flesh that's never had a man's callused hand touching it. It feels wonderful to be touched in such a way by him. He's gentle, but greedy. Hungry might be a better word.

I grabbed his hair causing that bandana to fall to the floor. "Oh my."

He let go of my left breast and reached down pushing my legs apart with his big hand. "Shh, be quiet." He ordered going back for the other nipple and sucking harder this time.

His fingers found me and I exploded immediately. "OH my God!!"

He came up and covered my mouth with his as he worked me up and over twice more.

When he let go and dropped to his knees I thought I'd fall with him. He shoved the skirt up making me squeak again.

He looked up and put his finger to his lips, "I said be quiet."

"I'm trying." I whispered.

"Try harder." He ordered and pressed his nose into the apex of my thighs.

My knees went out. Thankfully Lou caught me in his strong capable arms. I leaned back as he used his tongue to taste me a place that seems to explode at his will. I felt my body tremble again as his whiskers dug in against my thighs and his tongue probed deeper in search of of how wet he's made me.

He gave me one more good tongue lashing before helping me to the chair. "Good God woman."

I leaned back looking up at him. "That was your fault."

"Oh no, I'm not taking the blame for that one." He adjusted himself again. He rolled his eyes, "Pick what you like, surprise me." He meant the clothes and pulled the door shut behind him.

I stood up a second later and looked at myself in the mirror as I peel out of this crazy leather outfit he'd insisted I try on first. Now I know why. Sneaky bastard. I'll have to remember to give him a hard time tonight at dinner. A hard time. That is in fact what I'm giving him. I saw the bulge and the frustration on the poor man's face. Why do I feel so sorry for him? Because now I know what he wants. What his body wants. He wants me. I put my hand on the mirror to steady myself as the idea of such a big bad biker of a man wanting me, of all women, made me dizzy.

What would it be like to be naked and in this man's arms. It would be wonderful. I would kiss his tattoos and ask what they meant while he held me afterwards. As my body reacted and made me smile I forced the thoughts of making love to Lou aside. I don't know how, but the man has completely stolen my heart along with my senses.

I found a cute black and silver tight fitting dress that went very well with the thigh-high black leather boots. He'd tossed in some cute heels I would have worn any other day, but today, after what he just did, he's getting the boots. He all but said I was an uptight snob when we first met. In fact, I'm sure he came right out and used those exact words. Let's see how he deals with the sultry sexy Southern Belle I had no idea was inside me.

I pulled on the short matching jacket and checked myself. Not bad. Definitely better than the leather thing. I gathered the rest of the items before opening the door again.

This time I didn't give him a little show, I just handed him the clothes I wanted to purchase. "This should keep those wandering hands of yours preoccupied for a minute."

He bit his lip when he saw the boots. "Oh kitten, you're really going to kill me in those boots." He almost sounded like he was begging! Mission accomplished.

He paid for our purchases with his credit card.

I waited until we got back out into the main part of the mall. "You have to let me pay you back."

"For what?" He looked in the bag like a kid with a fresh bag of Halloween candy.

"Those."

"Why?" He looked at me with that wicked grin, "These are for me."

I rolled my eyes and laughed harder than I can remember laughing a very long time. "You're off your nut."

He put his hand on my lower back, "Geezus woman, you have every guy in here is drooling."

"You picked out the dresses."

"It's not the dress, well, yeah, it's the dress too, but it's you, in that dress and those boots. You're killing me!" He whispered in my ear.

"Good."

"Good?? Why good? Are you enjoying this??" He's completely surprised, and I'm loving every sweet second.

"You bet I am." I pointed to the Coach store. "Ooh purses, I need a purse since you made me leave my mine behind."

He's biting his knuckles trying to look at me and where we're walking at the same time. I think he's almost tripped twice.

I want to crack up so bad I might start shaking. "What's wrong? Hungry?" I said the last word very slowly.

He closed his eyes and bit harder.

I almost cried it was so perfect. He deserves this. Why? Because for the first time in my life I feel powerful and sexy. I know it's all his doing, but as this is all new to me, and not likely to last, so I'm going to enjoy every minute.

The look on Lou's face almost makes me feel sorry for him. Almost. I can't tell if he's still in shock, or just being silly, but he looks like he's going to implode as his eyes don't know whether to look up, or down.

I went into the store and found the bag I wanted fairly quickly. I know my Coach bags. This one is the newer model of the one I purchased over a year ago, but this time I purchased the black one. I love my camel colored bag at home, but black suites my new wardrobe much better these days.

Lou paid for this purchase too, despite my protests. I gave in because I didn't want to argue in front of the cashier.

We walked all over the mall before poor Lou couldn't take it anymore. "Babe, we need to get out of here."

I smiled sweetly up at him, "Why?"

"Because I'm about to kick every guy's ass in here. Dammit baby, I knew you would look hot, but you're tipping the scale here. Showing off is one thing, but now I'm getting possessive. We need to go." He insisted.

"One condition." I stopped in front of a shoe store just to taunt him.

He looked over my shoulder then back at me, "Anything, just don't go shoe shopping."

"It's my turn tonight."

He looked confused, beautifully befuddled. I think I just fell in love with him. "Your turn for what?"

I looked down and slowly back up.

"Oh, come on Barbara! I don't want to talk about this here."

"I wasn't looking to talk." I turned around. "I like those red heels in the window."

He growled and took my arm to turn me around, "Fine. Whatever you want. We're leaving."

"Promise?"

"Now look woman. This is important, I want to make this right for you."

"You don't get to have all the fun. It's not fair."

"What are you talking about?? Your'e the one having all the fun if I'm not mistaken!"

People are starting to look again. It made me smile. "Oh, so it's okay if you get to touch me, but I can't touch you?"

"BARBARA!!" He snapped a little too loud. Even I jumped a little.

"That's the deal. New shoes, or you let me play." I crossed my arms and tossed my hip out.

He narrowed his eyes, "We're leaving. Right now." He took me by the arm and started for the exit.

I pulled free but kept walking with him. He decided to take my hand, which is much more difficult for me to break free of.

It was a fast and furious walk back to the hotel room. My inner bitch is drumming her fingers on the table. This isn't over. I do not take kindly to being dragged about like a suitcase on wheels.

Once inside the room he all but threw the bags against the wall and started for me.

I backed up and used the table as a shield. "Problem Mr. Colson?"

He stopped and crossed his arms. "What the fuck were you doing back there?"

"Messing with you." I can't keep the smile from the corners of my mouth.

"Why?"

"Because you're being stubborn. Why can't I touch you?" The right words aren't quite there. This is new to me, but fun!!

He set his jaw before saying, "I told you how I wanted this to go. You deserve to be treated like the lady you are. I will NOT do this to you."

"Do what to me?"

He let out a frustrated breath. "What you're asking for should come later. After the . . . I don't know!! You shouldn't have to do that!!"

"I never said I felt like I had to. I said I wanted to. I don't even know how to do what I want to do to you, but you don't get to dictate how this whole thing goes. It is *my* virginity after all. You might be the big bad biker, but I will not be controlled."

"I'm not trying to control you! And that's just it! You don't know!"

"So you're afraid I'll do it wrong?"

He grabbed the back of the chair and flung it so hard it shattered against the kitchen bar. "FUCK!!!!" He spun around and left the suite putting a hole in the wall along the way.

"Well, that didn't go as planned." I sat in one of the non-shattered chairs and took off my boots. I wonder if he'll come back. Maybe I pushed him too far. I was trying to tell him it was okay, and that I wanted to . . . well, I suppose it doesn't matter now.

Maybe it's best he leaves. I'd hate to uproot his life and drop him in the middle of my bullshit.

The idea of him not coming back broke my heart into a thousand pieces. I put my head on the table and cried harder than I've ever cried in my entire life. I thought about losing Lou, my father, and possibly Myles. I mean seriously, I'm an adult now. Myles really should move on.

When the tear well dried up I went to the bathroom to take a shower. I want to wash everything off. Everything from the last week. Especially the last twenty minutes. I scrubbed and scrubbed, but it's not on the outside, it's on the inside.

I gave up and sat on the tile floor. I told myself I was going to shave my legs, but never picked up the razor. The water feels good. Warm. Soothing. I managed to get up and wash my face and condition my hair.

I dried off and found the hotel robe to hide under. I knew I wouldn't sleep. Not without Lou. Hell, if he doesn't come back I may never sleep again. I'm such an idiot.

I poured two fingers of whiskey and went to sit on the floor by the window in the main part of the suite. The sun is setting, but it's not quite down enough for the city lights to set in. I leaned my head against the wall and contemplated giving Paulie the eight million dollars.

It goes against every fiber of my being to give up like this, but I'm afraid the fight may be tapped out of me. I'm not a fighter. I don't know what I am.

I heard the door open but didn't have the guts to look. If I look it will be Myles and my disappointment will show on my face. That would be rude.

I felt him though. I know it's not Myles. I know Lou's presence without seeing him. Still, I kept my eyes on the horizon.

He sat next to me. "I'm sorry if I scared you. I shouldn't have demolished the chair like that."

"Fuck the stupid chair." I surprised myself with my vulgar snap. I think I've said that word one other time in my life, maybe twice. I still doesn't taste right on my tongue.

"Can you look at me please?" He begged.

"No." I wiped the corner of my eye whose tears betrayed my relief that he's back.

"I didn't mean to scare you. I would never lay a hand on you. You know that right?"

Now I had to look at him, "I know that!! I wasn't scared of you! I was scared you wouldn't come back."

"I yelled at you, smashed a chair to smithereens, and you're mad because you thought I wouldn't come back?"

"Not mad. Scared. Much worse." I swirled my drink and took a big sip.

"I would never leave you like that. I stepped out to cool off. I had it in my head how I wanted it to be. I want to make this right for you. I know how to seduce a woman, I don't know how to make her first time perfect. I want everything to be perfect for you." He explained sounding frustrated.

"Lou, if my first time is with you, it will be perfect. I just want to play first. Get to know each other. You get to touch me. I want the same in return."

He closed his eyes for a second then looked back at me, "Okay. I hadn't thought of it like that. What do you want to do?"

"Nothing now, you've destroyed the mood like you destroyed that chair." I stood up setting my now empty glass on the table and ruffing his hair. "Are you still taking me to dinner?"

"Are you going to wear those boots?" He turned and stood to pick up the remnants of the chair off the floor.

"Do you want me to?"

"No."

"Then I will not wear the boots." I stepped over to help him set the chunks of wood out of the way.

When we finished making our pile he cupped my face and set his forehead on mine. "I'm not good at this. I've never had a *real* relationship, not one I took seriously, and I've never been with a virgin."

"My virginity does not define me. I need you to listen to me. Don't just force things your way because you think that's what's best for me. I know what's best for me. I've done a damn good job so far of doing what's best for me." I assured him.

He lowered his chin and kissed me. "I'm sorry. I wanted so bad to make it all perfect for you."

"Then stop trying to control everything." I touched his beard that's getting longer and softer now. "Are you growing this in?"

"It was down to here." He put his hand to the base of his neck, "But I got caught in a fire, lost the beard and the hair."

"A fire??"

"Yeah, warehouse fire. It's a long story." His thumbs are on my cheeks. His eyes are stealing mine. "I love you Barbara. I love you so much." He insisted.

"I love you too." The words came to me so naturally I surprised myself. This word tasted much better on my tongue.

He lowered and kissed me slow and sweet for a few minutes. Then he lifted up and asked, "We okay?"

I nodded, "Probably better."

"I feel like I'm five." I laughed and leaned into him.

"You can't come to Vegas and not do the jousting show at least once."

I looked up and will never forget the love of my life, this big bad biker, wearing a king's crown made of paper. He almost looks royal, and he's all smiles. Not very royal behavior. "You're loving this!" I accused happily.

He looked back down and tucked me under his arm. He put his finger to his lips, "Shh. If the club finds out they'll beat my ass."

I laughed, "I seriously doubt that."

"You don't know Gunner." He laughed and kissed my forehead. "Alright, here we go. Don't forget we're the black knight, he almost always wins."

Lou didn't hoot and cheer like the rest of the audience, but he did clap and look to me often. I think he wants to make sure I'm having fun.

Truth be told, I *am* having fun! The knights are all so handsome with their long hair and fancy outfits. The tricks they perform in unison are very entertaining. The fake fighting could use some work, but hey, it's a kid's show. The red knight won tonight, but Lou didn't seem to care.

Afterwards we walked down the strip taking in the cool night air.

Lou felt me shiver when a breeze blew down the street and took his jacket off to help me into it. "This reminds me. Why did you take my cut with you into the bar that morning in Arizona?"

"I was cold. It was closer than my jacket. Why?" Uh oh. Here it comes.

"There's only two reasons a woman puts on a cut. One, he's picking her up off the side of the road and she needs protection for riding. And two, if she's his old lady." Red had already explained this, but it was nice to hear it from him.

I hugged myself in the warmth of the heavy leather. "Why do you call your wives 'old ladies'? It sounds horribly degrading."

"Not at all. When a man refers to a woman as his old lady that means he wants to grow old with her." He clarified.

"Well, as I have no intention of growing old gracefully, I would appreciate you not calling me that."

"It's a term of endearment. It means wife. I like you in my cut. You're the first to wear it besides myself."

"I am??"

"Yes my dear, I've told you, I don't date. It's been three years since my last half ass girlfriend, and she didn't hang around very long. She couldn't handle my being gone all the time." He explained. "The few so-called girlfriends I've had knew better than to try to wear my cut."

"If things settle down on my end, and you go back to work. Where does that leave me?" I changed the subject not wanting to talk about his ex-girlfriends any longer.

"I'll find work that doesn't take me away from home. Speaking of home. Since you can't go back to yours, do you want to come to mine? We should leave Vegas tomorrow."

"Where do you live?"

"Just outside Seattle in a town called Newcastle."

"Is it as cold and rainy as I've heard?"

"Probably, but now you have me and all your new leather riding gear to keep you warm." He hugged me to him.

Once back in our room I poured a glass of wine and sat by the window. The dinner and show took my mind off things for a while, but now it's getting crowded again inside my head. I have this strong need to put all of this behind me. To forget about Paulie and this money.

Lou sat down on the floor beside me with a beer, "You okay?."

I shrugged, "I feel guilty. I mean, my father, Mr. Whitmore, was never there for me unless it meant writing a check, but maybe I should send for his remains." I sipped my whiskey grateful for the strong flavor and Lou's presence to help me work through these thoughts.

"We have another problem." He started but let it hang waiting for me to catch up.

I looked over to him and turned so I could see him better. "Okay, I'm ready." I took a deep breath and another sip. "Tell me."

"As my old lady I'm going to protect you with every resource I have. That means involving my family, the club to be exact. We're talking about a full scale mob on club war. That hasn't happened in over ten years."

I sighed, "I can't just hand him over money that was not his to begin with. I can't help that my father botched a deal for him, and deal gone bad does not entitle him to compensation in this case."

"This could get very ugly over your pride." He argued.

"It's not pride, it's smart. If I let him bully me out of the eight million, then that opens me up to be bullied out of everything that's left of my father's empire. I don't care how Mr. Whitmore acquired his money, it's mine now. I'll clean my own house where it needs to be cleaned. I'll make the retributions where it's needed, but I won't just hand over that kind of money because he feels slighted."

"I understand your point, please tell me you heard what I said." He insisted.

"I heard you, and I get it. Lou, if you don't want the club involved, then don't get them involved. I can hire a security team, even some thugs if I have to. I won't hold it against you if you want to step away from this."

"Not an option. You're my old lady, and you'll be my wife. I'm just trying to talk some sense into you."

"I don't want to ruin a perfectly good evening. Can we fight about this tomorrow?"

His eyes darted over mine, "No. I'm afraid you're about to get really pissed off at me."

"Why?"

"I can't let you do this. Not just because you could start a war, but because it's too dangerous. I won't lose you my love. I'll take your anger over your death any day." He stood up.

"Where are you going?"

"To call Myles and have him take over your father's company in your place. I don't want you anywhere near those illegal businesses. When Myles sorts things out you can have it all back. By then we should have Paulie taken care of."

"You can't do that. It's my company, he can't make a move without my consent."

"I know, that's why you're going to hire him as CEO and give him the right to do whatever he wants."

"You can't force me to sign anything."

"If you don't give Myles CEO rights, you're going to get him killed."

I looked at him, "Are you blackmailing me??"

"Yes. Turn over the company, or put Myles at more risk than he already is. I won't back down on this, and I'm sure he'll agree. I'm sorry kitten, but you need to do what I tell you. Please." He's a little too calm.

I just sat there in shock. Did he just rip the rug out from under me? I believe he did. Now I'm trapped. Caged. Mad. Very, very mad. "I don't really want to see you right now."

"Are you asking me to leave?"

"No, just get out of my face before I punch you in yours." I really wanted to cry, but not in front of him. I don't want to be consoled, I want to go stark raving mad, alone.

He stood, "I'm sorry baby. This is the only way I know to protect you, and my family. I can't be responsible for a mob war. Not for you, not for anyone."

I closed my eyes. "Please stop talking to me."

"Alright. I'll be in the bedroom. I love you Barbara, please don't take that lightly, or forget it."

I turned to lean my forehead against the glass. I let the tears fall as soon as I sensed he was out of the room. Everything, gone. Just like that. One week ago I had everything. Income. A distant but caring enough father to see to my education and make sure I had a job wherever I wanted. A car. I was just getting used to life at home full-time when Lou showed up.

Now this. My real father is a mob enforcer, my boyfriend is a Transporter for this motorcycle club, Myles is God knows where, and I'm crying over the most beautiful lights in the country.

Lou wants to marry me. I don't think so, not after this. I suppose I could just sell everything off, pay the eight million dollars, and put a stop to all this. No. That's not me. I won't be bullied like that. But my pride will start a war. I never asked for Lou's help!! Why can't he just . . . what? Walk away?

I remember that feeling. It sucked. I have a choice to make. My pride, or Lou. This has to be my choice, or I'll resent him. I love him, but resentment can burn low and slow, destroying a relationship. So I've read.

I stood up and jumped a little when I saw him leaning on the door frame leading into the bedroom. "You scared me. Have you been standing there the whole time?"

He shrugged. "Only after I talked to Myles for a minute."

"Look, we need to talk about this."

"Talk." His mood is about as dark as mine right now.

"I'll sell everything, and pay the eight million. Whatever is left I'll find something else to do with it. This can't be your decision, it has to be mine."

He nodded, "That works just fine for me. Let Myles sell everything off. I don't want you anywhere near those companies or the money."

"I hardly see how it matters whether I do it or not, Paulie still gets the money." I argued.

"I told you, I don't want you anywhere near Mr. Whitmore's bullshit. If he's got shady companies, and it sounds like he does, you could get in serious trouble. Let Myles handle it." He insisted.

"You're ripping the rug out from under me Lou, and I have to tell you, I do not like it one bit."

"I know. I'd apologize, but I'm not sorry. I'm going to protect you if it's the last thing I do." He vowed.

"I don't need your protection, I have Myles and his security team." I argued and walked over to plop on the couch and pick up the remote.

"Am I allowed to come sit with you?"

"Why are you asking me?? You're going to do whatever you want anyway!" I flipped the channels hoping there is something on that will help calm my temper.

He sat down at the other end of the couch and settled in the corner with his left arm on the side and right across the back. Then he set his ankle on his knee. "How long are you going to be mad?"

"Until I'm not." I snapped.

"I'm assuming if I try to justify my actions it's only going to make things worse?"

"Yes. I believe if you were to stop talking for a while I might not throw something at you."

He just sat there watching me flip channels.

It was unnerving. "Stop staring at me."

"I can't. The way you looked at me over there is embedded in my brain. It's killing me kitten."

"Good. I don't like being bullied, or controlled in your case. And I really hate it when you're right."

He sat still in his little corner for a little while longer.

Then suddenly he shifted and put his head in my lap.

I looked down and sighed, "Don't try to be cute. I'm very mad at you."

"Do you understand why I'm doing this?"

I resisted the urge to let my fingers play in his unruly hair. "I understand you're worried about my safety, but that was not the way to handle it."

"Probably not, but I don't know another way."

"You could have talked to me."

"You weren't listening, and you were talking about endangering the lives of a lot of people. People I care a great deal about. I couldn't allow it."

"I'm still not very happy with you."

"That's a step up from mad as hell." He found my hand and put it under his on his chest.

"I don't like feeling trapped."

"You feel trapped?"

"I feel like everything is out of my control. I'm always in control."

"I'm sorry baby. I wasn't trying to trap you, or make you feel helpless. If you want to help Myles from Seattle over the phone, you can." He sounded like he was giving me permission.

"Gee thanks Master." I complained and smacked him lightly in the face with a couch pillow.

He smiled. "I could get used to you calling me Master."

I smacked him harder. "You wish."

"I don't like it when you're mad at me."

"Good, serves you right for taking everything away from me."

"I didn't do it to hurt you."

"Which is the only reason I haven't kicked your big butt to the floor."

"So, you get it?" He asked again obviously still concerned.

I melted, poor guy really does love me. He's been stalking me for half an hour for forgiveness. "Yes, I suppose I get it. Next time you think about doing something like this, I want you to talk to me first."

"I'll try, but I'm not so sure you would have listened. You're a stubborn little southern belle."

"And you're a controlling biker with eyes that make me melt. It's truly unfair of you to use them like weapons you know."

"Weapons?"

"Yes. I shouldn't be telling you this, but that's why I couldn't look at you earlier. You disarm me with those baby blues." I confessed.

"Good to know. Quite honestly you have the same effect on me." He reached up and tucked my hair behind my ear. "I love you Barbara. Are we okay?"

"Well, you're still in the dog house, but I'm not quite as mad as I was before."

"So, getting you naked is probably out?"

"It most certainly is." I decided trying to keep the smile from my lips.

"That's too bad. I bet you could go for a little stress relief."

"I'm quite enjoying my anger right now."

He cocked his eyebrow, "Really?"

I tugged a lock of his hair with my free hand. "I refuse to give you the pleasure, especially since you won't let me play." I reminded him.

7

"Are we really going back to that?" He sighed and I could tell he was losing his patience with me.

"Well? Why are you so stubborn?"

"Because I want it to be perfect for you. I told you that earlier."

"How do you know what's perfect for me? Maybe perfect for me is being able to give you what you give me." I'm having a hard time with the right words here.

He sat up and turned to face me, "Okay, obviously I need to be more clear. You're a beautiful, smart, sexy, virgin. You deserve to be treated like a princess, not have me making a mess all over you."

I felt my face heat up as I blushed. The idea of him in the throw of passion quickened my pulse.

"Are you smiling??" He asked lifting my chin. "Barbara. What's so funny?"

"Not funny, intriguing."

He studied my face and searched my eyes for a few seconds. "How far do you want to go? Maybe if you tell me I won't feel like such a pervert."

"Why do you feel like a pervert?" I truly don't understand.

"I'm a man having some seriously sexy thoughts about a proper lady. I shouldn't be thinking about your naked body and all that hair on my chest while you sit on."

I put my finger to his lips silencing him, "Okay, I get the idea."

He took my hand and kissed the back. "Again I ask, for Barbara?"

"I'm not on birth control, and I don't trust condoms."

"Okay, we'll take care of that. You should know that I'm planning to marry you, so no condoms. I don't want anything between us. I can wait for the birth control to kick in. There're plenty of other things we can do to get to know each other." He reasoned, then grinned a very sexy evil grin.

"Will you stop dictating how everything goes between us in that bed?" I nodded to the bedroom.

He gave me that wicked smile that warms my heart, "Can I dictate just a little?" He made that thumb and finger gesture meaning 'a little'.

I laughed and crawled into his lap for a hug. "Okay, but turn about is fair play. You're not the only bossy one in this relationship." I sat back and looked at him. Did you say you wanted to marry me?"

He stood taking me with him in his long strong arms. "That I did. Maybe if you let me out of that bed in time we can go find you a ring before we leave tomorrow."

"I haven't said yes yet." He is kidding, right??

He set me on the bed, "I'll ask with a ring in my hand."

"Where are you going?"

"I'm going to turn off the television in the other room and get some waters. You've been drinking too much lately. Probably my fault." He complained and left.

I rolled my eyes and turned the covers down. I thought about going to freshen up, but Lou is already back and setting glasses of water on the night stands. When he finished he walked over and shut the large double doors with one swing of his large wingspan.

The devilish grin is back as he looks at me, he's still lingering at the door.

"What are you doing way over there?"

He took two steps and launched himself on the bed at me. I screamed as he tickled and wrestled me under him. The grin is back as he hovers with me pinned and panting under him. "I love you Barbara. You know that?"

I played in his maturing beard and tilted my head, "How do you know you love me?"

"Do you want the short list, or the long list?"

"You have lists?"

"I do." He gummed my fingers as they passed his lips.

"I want the long list."

He slid off to his elbow beside me and put his hand flat on my stomach. His eyes stayed on his hand as his thumb moved back and forth. "I've dealt with a lot of people in my time. So many in fact no matter what they do it fails to surprise me. You surprise me at every turn." He looked up now and untucked my shirt. "I look into your eyes and I wonder what you're thinking, because I'm sure it's something that will throw me off guard. Don't get me started on your body. I've had three fashion shows from you in the last week and I can't decided which is more beautiful. The southern belle, the sexy short skirt Vegas goddess, or the comfortable jeans and sweater look."

"I like jeans." I giggled as he popped the button on the ones I'm wearing.

He smiled and kissed my nose. "Don't interrupt, I'm not done yet. You said you wanted the long list. Be patient." He scolded playfully.

"Yes dear. Please go on. I didn't mean to interrupt you." I replied too politely playing back.

He slid the zipper down as he continued, "The way you kiss me back drives me wild. You have all this uninhibited passion once you give in to me. I like that I have to try, to work to get you to melt. It makes me feel like a man. One that wants to feel that everyday for the rest of my life. You make me feel alive." He paused to kiss along my jaw and work my jeans down.

I helped by trying to kick out of them, he'd pushed them down so they're tangled around my feet. Seeing my struggle, he laughed, then moved down to remove them. He quickly pulled them off, then started kissing my feet, then kissed and nibbled all the way up my legs, stopping just before he reached that part of me. Then laid down next to me again.

He's looking down at the pink lace boy shorts I'd picked up during our shopping spree. He ran his finger just under the soft silky fabric. "Then there's the way you smell. I want to coat my beard with your juices so I can smell you all day long."

I smiled and nuzzled his chest with my nose. "That was a little graphic."

"Maybe, but it's true." He bent down and kissed my stomach. "I told you I was a pervert."

"Don't put words in my mouth. I said it was graphic, not perverted. I'm getting to like the way your words make me blush." I admitted feeling like I should offer up something since he's offering up this long list of why he loves me. I can't imagine a sweeter way to learn about intimacy with a man.

"I like making you blush. Your pale white skin turns a soft reddish pink that reminds me of soft pink roses." He moved down the bed and pulled my panties down. I lifted my knees to help him get them off.

I was more than a little surprised when he sat up and took my hand to draw me up with him.

Then he tugged my shirt. "Take it off. I want to see you."

I pulled the shirt off, then the bra a little slower than I meant to. his eyes are fun to watch as he takes me in and places kisses between glances and words along my neck and should. I tossed the clothing to the floor as he kissed me onto my back. I worked his shirt off when he let me up for air.

He stopped to look down at me as his fingers walked and tickled their way down. "I love everything about you Barbara. Everything in me wants to give you all the love you deserve in this life. I want to be the first thing you think about and see every morning, and the last at night as you fall asleep in my arms. I could go on for days about all the things I love about you, but right now what I really want to do is touch you. Taste you. Memorize every inch of you, then drive you wild with one orgasm after another until you scream my name and beg for me to make love to you."

"I thought I would be more nervous, but after the dressing room adventure, this feels pretty tame."

He smiled and I knew there was not only a lover on top of me, he was my friend. Someone I could talk to, joke with, and learn from. Everything I know about intimacy is being taught by Lou. I want to know more. I want to know everything he wants from me, so I can give it, and love him back.

"It won't feel so tame in a minute. I do appreciate a good challenge, and you my love, have been a challenge from day one." He kissed his way south.

Anticipation built up as the warmth of his chest against mine left me for tender kisses and little nips. I lost my grip on his shoulders and grabbed the sheets when he parted my legs. He touched me with his finger first. "Miss me baby?" He sucked his finger clean and my head fell back. I can't watch!!

His tongue was next as it gently explored driving me to the brink. Then he slowed taking me back down.

I felt pressure at my core as he asked, "May I?"

I nodded nervously biting my lip.

"It's going to hurt a little at first. I'll be gentle. Tell me to stop any time. Okay?"

I nodded again unable to look at him.

He kissed the inside of my thigh and began working his finger gently into me. I felt a bit of pressure, and a very slight pinch of pain. Everything is so wet down there. I can't believe that's just me. I feel so, brazen.

"Now for a little fun." He said in a soft husky voice. He moved out, and all the way in, then out, and back in. "Okay honey?"

I nodded eagerly pushing back for more. "Again."

"Shit." He cussed and I felt his teeth bite into my flesh as he groaned.

I propped up on my elbows and asked. "Are you okay?"

He shook his head and laughed as he looked up at me, "You just made me come in my pants."

"You did??" I smiled bigger than I should have because having such an effect on a man like Lou is so flattering it floors me. I've never felt so, sexy. I've never felt sexy period.

"I did. What are you smiling about??" He's trying to look offended, but the knowing little grin tells me he knows exactly how I feel right now. I find it interesting that such an emotion can go both ways. It's created another layer to our new evolving bond.

I put my head back down and covered my face, "You overwhelm me with your compliments."

"Let's see if can overwhelm you with something else." He picked up his previous rhythm and I was quickly lost in a sea of sensations I had no idea existed. It's like he's using my body as a musical instrument with my moans another musical note as the music builds.

I called mercy after the fifth, or was it sixth. I've lost track, but I know i'm getting a little sore, and if we still have to ride tomorrow I don't want to be terribly uncomfortable. I remember scolding him for purposely wearing me out so I wouldn't have the energy to argue with him about letting me touch him.

He just trapped my wandering hands in his, tucked me into his shoulder and wrapped the comforter around us and kissed the top of my head. "Sleep my little angel."

We must not have closed the curtains in the bedroom last night because a bright glaring light woke me up. When I blinked my eyes open trying to focus I realized the sun is up and reflecting proudly off the glass from another hotel room right into ours.

When I tried to move I had to laugh because the big heavy man I fell in love with so quickly is almost completely on top of me.

As I watched him sleep I wondered what his home is like in Washington. Does he have a house? An apartment? What does the inside look like? Is it bare, or decorated with a bunch of girly magazines and motorcycle parts? I can picture him on a ratty old couch rebuilding some greasy part with the television blaring classic rock from across the room.

I moved his hair off his face and tilted my head to see if he's asleep. He's so peaceful. He's a lot different like this than when he's angry, or worried to the point of snapping at me. Part of me likes knowing I can affect him so intensely. The other part would much rather see him like this.

He moaned waking up because I'm playing in his beard.

"It's morning." I whispered.

He hugged me under the weight of his body. "Mmmm. I like waking up with breakfast in bed."

I laughed because he's tickling my side and kissing my neck.

"Oh yeah, I could get used to this." He nipped along my jaw and ran his hand down my side and to my thigh.

"No, it's my turn." I closed my legs and rolled to my side taking away his 'breakfast'. "I don't want to argue with you before coffee. Lay back." I gave him a little poke in the shoulder.

He groaned and rolled to his back keeping his boxers on and put his hands behind his head. "Be gentle."

I sat up and hooked the hem of his shorts with my fingers until his long hard shaft appeared tip first. I wondered for a second if it would ever end as I tugged the elastic down over his butt.

When I slid up to touch him with my nose it jumped.

I squealed then laughed, "Hey!! Did you do that?" I looked up at him.

He gave me a look that told me he was guilty.

I rolled my eyes, "Be nice."

He laughed and let his head fall back. "Take me in your hand, not your mouth."

"What did I tell you about dictating?" I flicked his tip with my tongue having settled into a nice position on his hip to play. His skin is soft, but he's very firm underneath.

"I don't want to come in your mouth." he breathed as I tried to see if his tip would fit in my mouth. It did, barely. I relaxed my jaw and backed off to lick the swollen tip. "Shit." He's panting and pulling the sheets up off the bed. I think I heard one rip.

I let my hand slide down to explore the soft sack with the light spray of hair.

His butt lifted up off the bed almost poking me in the eyes. "STOP!!"

I laughed and waited until he was under control. "Ticklish?"

He laughed and smacked his face with the palm of his hand then holding it there. "I'm going to hell for this."

"Nah, you have me to redeem you." I gently took my grip on his shaft again and lifted his tip to my lips. I licked the little bit of wet off the end and ran him across my lower lip, then my upper.

"Not your mouth, just your hand."

"Will you hush already?" And to silence him I tightened my grip and closed my mouth over as much of him as I could take. Talk about a feeling of power. Lou all but hit the roof, and I know I heard sheets ripping this time.

He put his hand on my shoulder and begged me to stop, but I didn't want to. I wanted him. I wanted to taste him like he'd tasted me. His protest fell on deaf stubborn ears as I took the last of his resolve. I swallowed letting his flavor linger on my tongue as I made sure to get it all.

When I looked up I laughed and kissed his hip. Poor guy has a pillow over his face and his knuckles are almost white. "Are you okay? Did I do something wrong?" I knew I hadn't, but I couldn't resist his reaction.

He tossed the pillow to the floor and lifted his head, "You're kidding right?"

I curled up into his shoulder and lifted the torn sheet, "Bret is not going to be happy with you."

"That's nothing new. At least this way he'll know something really wonderful happened in his bed, and I'll never tell him what. The torture comes in the not knowing and always left wondering."

"You're mean."

"You're beautiful. Thank you baby, but you shouldn't have done that

"Will you hush already?" I interrupted him rudely, but he is being stubborn, and downright silly at this point. "I had fun, don't scold me for it."

He groaned in protest but let it drop. I smiled and kissed his chest then I heard him snoring lightly. And he said he didn't sleep well away from the club.

Lou was on the phone and pacing the living area when I'd finished taking a shower and getting dressed. He was already up and gone when I woke up, so I'd scampered off to the bathroom feeling suddenly naked. Funny how I didn't feel so naked last night, or this morning.

I stood in the doorway watching him pace and rake his hand through his hair.

"I know, just take care of it . . . No . . . Alright, send the paperwork to my Seattle P.O. Box, and tell Bret I shit on his pillow." He hung up.

I felt my jaw drop. "You did what?"

He laughed and tossed the phone hard onto the dining room table. I hope he didn't break it. "Not really. It's a running joke. About three months ago I did a job for one of the Utah chapters, Dingos I believe. Anyway, I needed to borrow one of Bret's cars, which is normal, except the only one he had was one in which one of his whores had thrown up in the night before.

"Not only had he neglected to tell me this, but I thought he was getting me back for wrecking one of his boats last year. We've been going back and forth like this for about four years. I drove one of his cars off a bridge onto a lake one time. My version of a car wash.

"Three weeks ago I came home from helping some friends move. I'd taken my truck, so the bike was in the garage. That fucker had somebody take my bike apart and reassemble it upright in the shower stall inside my house."

I put my hand to my mouth to try and hide my giggle, "That's brilliant."

He shrugged, "I kind of thought so. Anyway, that's why I told him I shit on his pillow."

"What paperwork were you talking about?" I asked picking bacon off a tray. He must have ordered breakfast while I was still sleeping. How long has he been up?

"Bret's lawyer is also my lawyer, do me a favor, and never mention that. Okay?"

"Why?"

"Because Bret is the asshole half brother we all hate. A few of us can handle him, but the rest, not so much. He went after Joe's wife, Red, a while back. I'm still not sure why Bret is alive after that stunt." He picked up a sausage link to wiggle at me as he looked me over. "Those boots work very well with those jeans."

"I figured they would work as chaps. The chaps are nice, but it's supposed to be hot today. I thought the boots would be a little cooler." I've learned a few things after a week of hanging around with bikers.

"Close enough." His eyes discovered cleavage. "You better put a jacket on."

"I have a jacket."

He's still eyeing me funny.

"What?"

He walked over and picked up the string of the leather corset at my cleavage. Ever since I've started wearing this corset like leather vest my breasts seem huge.

"I thought we had to leave." I looked for his eyes, but they're intent on his task.

He loosened the strings and hooked his finger creating lower cleavage. He ran his thumbs over my nipples moving the fabric out of the way and came down for a good taste on each before fixing my top. This time it's much looser.

"Let's get out of here before I have to get dressed twice in one morning." He kissed my cheek.

"Good idea."

"Do you live in an apartment?" I asked picturing the bachelor pad again.

"Nope, I have a house. It's nothing fancy, but you can fix that."

"As long as we don't have to stay in another hotel."

He laughed, "Don't worry, no more hotels for you when this is over, unless you want to that is. It depends on where you want to go for our honeymoon. I built the house, so you're stuck with it unless you really hate it."

"You built a house?" I asked as he secured the bags on the backrest.

"Yeah, I was bored and work was slow. I put a lot into the construction of the house, but not so much the decor. I'm sure you can handle that part for us." There he goes again talking about marriage. He righted his bike and helped me on behind him. "Ready baby?"

For what? Marriage, or you in general? I think that's a topic for another time. "How far is this ride?"

"We'll stop in Boise, it's about an eight hour ride. I just need to stop for gas otherwise we'll try to ride straight through. Tomorrow is another eight hours to Seattle. It's going to be a lot of riding for two days, if it gets too much let me know and we'll break the trip up some more."

"How long can you normally ride?"

"I can ride for a good eighteen hours only stopping for fuel and food. That's why I said let me know if you get sore or need to stop."

"Okay, let's go! I want to see this house you built!!" I sat back and let my fingers untuck his shirt under his leather jacket so I can feel the softness of his skin.

He backed us from the parking space and started the roaring engine before pulling us easily out onto the strip. Twenty or so minutes later I saw the sign for the 15

North. I stopped paying attention to the street signs after that and just looked at the scenery around me.

Riding is becoming more familiar now. When I'm not looking at the passing horizon I'm studying the patches on the back of his jacket. It's wickedly cool, vicious, but well done. It seems angry with the skulls and snakes, but men like that kind of stuff. It needs a nice red rose right there. I traced my finger along the bottom.

I got bored a few hours later and started working my hands around to his front. I want to touch him again. He leaned back a little giving my fingers room to move. I wasn't really trying to do anything, but I couldn't help myself. Maybe I'll just touch him. I bet it would feel good to hold him so intimately while we ride the open road.

Then again I should behave. He *is* driving after all. I stopped my progress and just let my fingers play just under his waistband and only down to where the patch of hair starts.

He found a straight clear lane and settled in to take one hand off the handle bars and put it over mine. I think that means I'm okay to be here. I gave him a little hug and went back to sight seeing.

Time flies pretty quickly on the back of a bike when you get used to it. We'd stopped for greasy burgers at lunchtime, but otherwise kept on riding. Lou asked me a couple times if I was okay, and as far as I can tell, I'm pretty darn good! My rump is a little flat and sore, but years of sitting in classes has me pretty well versed in the art of sitting for hours on end.

It was after dark before we stopped again. This time I'm done for sure. First of all I don't want to ride at night.

I looked up and saw the sign, Hotel 43? If I remember correctly this is one of the nicest hotels in the country. I remember reading about it in one of my travel magazines.

Lou helped me off the bike and shut the engine down. He pulled his leg over and stood upright instantly reminding me just how big he is.

He took my hand and pulled me over so I have to look up at him. He removed his sunglasses and set those beautiful blue eyes on mine. "While you were sleeping this morning I called and booked a suite here. It's one of the fancier places I could get into at the last minute. They have a spa if you'd like a massage tomorrow."

I jumped up and wrapped my arms around his neck and kissed him as hard as I could. He tastes so good.

Somehow I know this is the only man who tastes this good. His hands are strong and capable on my back.

He grabbed my butt with both of those big hands making me pull back in surprise. "Lou!! People can see us!"

He raised his eyebrow a little and tilted his head, "You jumped me."

"You really booked this fancy place?" I looked around.

"I did. I want to spend a couple nights here. Maybe go look for wedding rings in town tomorrow." He set me back on my feet. "I like you this happy."

"I like being this happy. Now I know why you didn't mention the rings this morning."

He shrugged, "After I thought about it I didn't want the ring to remind you of all that went down in Vegas."

"I don't think it would have mattered, but I was anxious to leave there. I found myself looking over my shoulder for Paulie, it was unsettling."

A valet stepped over pulling a luggage cart, "Can I get your bags?"

Lou was still focused on me, "Yes." He held the keys out to the kid. "Can you park her without dropping her?"

"Yes sir, my father rides, taught me well. If you just step inside, I'll see to your things." He assured us.

I can't take my eyes off Lou's. "You're going to let him ride your bike?"

He shrugged, "Normally, no, but I'm making an exception today. I don't want to leave your side just yet." He put his arm around my shoulders and led me inside.

"I think I'll be okay if you want to go park your bike." I tried to assure him.

"I'm sure you would be, but I'm not taking any chances until we get to Newcastle." He handed Sheila behind the counter a credit card and I'm assuming his ID.

She beamed up at him, "Mr. Colson! Welcome to Hotel 43. Would you still like dinner served at nine?"

"Yes, and make sure there's two bottles of champagne. Did you get the rest of my requests?" He hinted making my eyebrows go up. What's he up to??

"Yes sir. The list was very clear, and we were able to handle it without a problem." She motioned to another young man in a fancy hotel suit. "Kenrick here will show you to your suite. Mrs. Colson?" She looked at me now.

I blinked and had to muster a little Charm to reply, "Yes?"

"Your husband asked that we put you on a waiting list for the spa. I have two openings, one at ten and another at one. Would you like a massage or manicure?"

I looked at my nails, "Well, I'll take the ten for a mani-pedi if that's okay?"

She smiled, "Certainly. You can have the one o'clock for a massage if you'd like." She hinted.

"Um, no. Thank you. The mani-pedi will be more than enough." The only reason I'm bothering is because they're due, and I want to look my best for meeting Lou's Newcastle family.

"I'll schedule you in. Have a pleasant evening Mr. and Mrs. Colson." She batted her lashes and blushed when she looked at Lou.

I felt my eyes roll as we followed Kenrick to the elevators. "If that woman drooled any more she'd need a bib."

Lou laughed, "It's the eyes. Women love blue eyes. At least that's what I've come to understand."

"Oh, it's the eyes, but that's not all. Your hair is unruly. Like you just woke up. Then you add to it the fact that you look like you could bench press a stagecoach and it's no wonder women drool over you." I remembered the bell hop as we stepped into the elevator and felt myself blush a little at my bold words.

"I've never tried a stagecoach, but Joe and I picked up a Volkswagen a couple months ago."

"Pray tell, why were you lifting a car?"

"It was stuck in a ditch. It didn't seem right to rip the fender off, and possibly the wheel, when it was otherwise just a little banged up. It was sitting like this," he showed me his hand at an odd angle, "so we picked it up and carried it out instead of yanking it out with a wench."

"Wow. That is quite impressive." I knew he was strong, but car carrying strong?? Wow.

"Not really. Joe probably could have done it himself. Turner definitely could have. I was just trying to help, and maybe showing off a little. It doesn't hurt a man's

reputation to have rumors of car lifting floating around."
He kissed the top of my forehead.

I watched as the bellhop measured his own bicep
with his hand and looked up at Lou, "Maybe I should hit
the gym."

Lou laughed enjoying himself, "If you do, start with
some kickboxing. It'll make you strong and fast. Weights
are for pussies, if you're going to work out, work it out,
don't fuck around. Make sure you run too. Sometimes
you need to be able to run."

He nodded, "Yes sir. I'll do just that."

I felt my eyes roll again as I hugged Lou around his
waist. "You're going to have him riding motorcycles and
picking up chicks before we get out of this elevator."

The elevator doors opened saving him from having
to reply.

"Right this way folks. I took the liberty of filling the
hot tub. It will stay warm on it's own, so take your time
getting settled in." He opened a large door and led us
to the main living area of a large apartment. Suites are
big, this is more like an apartment. I like the reds and
browns of the decor. The furniture is contemporary, but
still manages to be warm.

"It's lovely." I turned and almost jumped as Lou
handed me a glass of champagne.

"As are you my love." He tapped his glass to mine
and held it up in toast. "Here's to Myles. He just sent me
a text a few minutes ago. Evidently he bought a FatBoy
in Vegas and is headed this way."

"He bought what??"

"A motorcycle baby, a Harley. I told him where we were going and he said he'll see us at the Newcastle chapter when we get there. Sounds like he hit it off pretty well with the guys in Vegas."

I took a sip before saying, "I have no idea what you just said." I laughed because I really don't have a clue what he's talking about, and don't much care. If Myles is happy, than so am I.

"Myles is coming up to move closer to you. To us. He wants to take care of your father's fallout where he can keep an eye on you." He teased.

"Won't he be tripping over you?"

"No. I'm going to see how he fits in with the club. If I'm right he's going to be busy prospecting for the next year. The club could use a man with his skill set."

"Don't you get him in any trouble." I warned him.

"Myles can take care of himself." He countered.

"He still works for me." I argued.

"Will you quit worrying?? You're supposed to be drinking champagne and eyeing that hot tub in the bathroom." He urged.

I sighed giving in. I can't help it. He's right, I really do need to stop worrying. Myles has taken care of me, and himself, my entire life.

"Why don't you go do that now." He suggested as he turned away.

"You sound like you're trying to get rid of me."

"I need to make a few calls before we settle in for the night."

"Kiss me first?"

"Always."

My glass was just about empty when Lou walked in the bathroom. I'd put some shampoo in the tub so the jets made a nice blanket of bubbles covering me.

I couldn't control the smile that took over my face as he sat on the floor facing me and topping off my champagne. "Myles will be arriving at the club tomorrow afternoon or evening. He wants you to call him tomorrow."

"He does?"

"He wants to hear it from you that I'm keeping my hands to myself." He looked at me knowingly.

"Myles can smell a lie, even through a telephone. I think I'd be better served to tell him we're engaged."

"I wonder if he'll tell you it's too fast like any father would."

"Probably, but we can be engaged for a while. No need to rush getting married."

"I suppose not, but don't think for one second you're getting out of marrying me." He picked up a beer and drank from the bottle.

"Champagne not your style?" I sipped mine thinking it's a good thing supper is coming soon. I don't want this champagne to go to my head.

"Not especially." He leaned his head back against the wall and looked up at the ceiling.

"Are you alright?"

"I told Slider about Paulie, and the possible fallout. He's not real happy, but he's going to alert the rest of the club in case the mob starts sniffing around for you."

"I really don't want to start a war."

"It may not come to that. With Slider involved there may be another solution. Sometimes I forget just how far he can reach with the club behind him."

"You still sound worried."

"People come to me for protection, I'm not used to asking the club for help, at least not on this large of a scale."

"What about Turner? You asked him for help."

"Sort of. I had something I needed to give him, and since he rarely makes an appearance I called him in on the job. A few years ago we used to run regular jobs together. Six or seven times a year. Lately he's become more distant. I haven't seen him in about a year."

"Maybe Georgia will be good for him."

He laughed, "She already is. I didn't tell you earlier in case you slipped up and said something, but he calls her Peach."

I laughed almost spilling my champagne. "He does??? He talks to her??"

"Well, yes, he talks to her. Only her as far as I know, but he signed it that way a couple times when he referred to her during the road trip. Georgia sent me an apology text for you today." He added.

"She doesn't owe me an apology! I owe her one!!" I popped the drain. "Can you start the shower? I want to rinse and dry off before I turn into a prune."

He stood and reached into the shower stall. "She understands what you did, so does everyone else. Don't worry about it. You did nothing wrong."

"I still feel like I betrayed her." I replied. "I know you've . . . seen me . . . but can I get a couple minutes here?"

He smiled and flipped on the towel warmer before leaving me to my nightly routine. "Take your time love."

I took my time just like he said. It wasn't easy. For some strange reason I miss him! I laughed at myself because I know he's in the other room.

The bath and shower revitalized me from the long day of riding. I should pick up a camera for tomorrow's ride. Speaking of cameras, where's my phone? And my wallet?? When I called home before I didn't have a forwarding address, now I know I can use Lou's.

I went to find Lou who is just shutting the main door behind him. "Did you leave?"

"No, the guy just finished setting up dinner." He pointed to a candle lit dinner set up on the large table.

"Wow." There are real plates and silver. The flowers are exploding with color just off center so when we sit we can see each other from across the table. "Suddenly I could eat a horse."

He walked over and pulled a chair out motioning for me to sit, "My lady. I hope you like lobster."

"Doesn't everyone?" I smiled up at him, "Thank you Lou, this is very sweet. I love it."

He bent down and kissed my cheek, "You are most welcome. Have a seat." He gestured to the chair with his hand.

I took my seat and let him push me in as I picked up my napkin.

He sat across from me. "Please tell me you have something on under that robe." He said before removing the silver domes covering our plates revealing lobster, mashed potatoes and long slender carrots.

"Of course I do. It's chilly in here." I waited as he poured wine into our glasses. "I thought you didn't care for wine?"

"I like it just fine. I prefer a good cold beer, but I'm going with the moment." He smiled that sweet soothing smile that tugs at my heart.

"If you would rather have a beer, I wish you would have one. We're supposed to be getting to know each other. How will I know what you really like if you're 'going with the moment' and not being yourself?" I picked up the wine and waited for him to lift his. "Thank you Lou, for the lovely hotel, the beautiful room, and most of all for sticking with me during this crisis."

He tapped his glass to mine, "I'd like to be at your side for all your ups and your downs."

I smiled before taking a sip and setting the glass down to focus on the food. "I may just take you up on that."

"I should hope so, we're buying wedding rings tomorrow." He took a bite of his lobster.

I laughed enjoying the flavor of my own lobster now. We were both too hungry to do any more talking until we sat back with full bellies.

"Now I'm tired again." I said picking up my wine as I looked across the table to the man I have fallen so hard and fast in love with I still can't believe it's real.

"I have one more surprise for you first, then you can sleep whenever you're ready." He said suspiciously.

"What did you do?" I've never been surprised like this. If you had asked me two days ago if I like surprises, I would have said no. But now, here, with Lou and that boyish grin gracing his lovely face . . . I love surprises.

He leaned over and pulled a gift wrapped box from the seat next to him. I hadn't noticed it, but then again it was under the table. He slid it across the table towards me.

"I come through this town a lot in my travels, so I have a few friends here in town. I called my buddy Termite and asked for a favor. He said his wife, Mary, had already gotten a call from Liz and would take care of it. She's one of the nicest old ladies I've met. We might be having lunch with them tomorrow if you would like." He seemed to be rambling uncomfortably.

I touched the big silver ribbon on the present. Tears filled my eyes as I suddenly realized this is the first time anyone has ever given me a present. A wrapped present.

"Baby?? Are you okay??" Lou leaned over and put his hand on mine.

I gripped his hand and sniffed, "My first present!" I laughed feeling like I sound ridiculous. He probably thinks I'm a sap.

He stood up and came around to pull me up into his embrace. "Oh honey. How could you have gone your whole life without one present?"

"Myles gives me flowers. He doesn't do gifts." I justified.

"I'm sure he wouldn't know what to get the woman who has everything."

I looked up stepping back, "That's what I always thought. I used to pretend they were from some secret admirer, but don't tell him that."

He smiled and touched his thumbs to my cheeks as he held my face, "Never. From now on you'll get flowers all the time, and that admirer will be me."

"Can I open it now?" The excitement is taking over the shock.

He lowered and kissed me sweetly before stepping back and pulling me into his lap as he sat in my chair. "Make sure you rip the paper."

I picked up the box. "It's heavy."

"A bunch of the old ladies got together and came up with their own patch. It's a feminine version of ours. I thought Slider was going bust a vein, but he approved it in the end. When I told Liz, about you she called Mary and had one brought over to the hotel for you. I might have let it slip you were a little nervous and might feel out of place surrounded by a bunch of bikers."

I ripped open the box wondering how a patch could be so heavy. I glanced at Lou before pulling the top off the box. "This is fun."

He laughed, "Good. I'll have to remember to get you presents with big fancy bows more often. That smile is incredible."

I set the lid aside and almost choked up. Sitting there in the box is a beautiful patch of colors that make up the feminine version of the patch on the back of Lou's jacket. Or cut, as I'm learning it's referred to as.

I studied the image with my fingertip tracing the outline of the motorcycle and the long blonde hair flowing from the rider. She's wearing a bandana and sunglasses, but you can see she's pretty. Sexy pretty.

The flames licking up from the bottom told the story of riding through hell. Two snakes wound up around a cross with a soaring eagle that make it look like he's following her. Protecting her.

"It's perfect. Beautiful, and intimidating." I lifted the black leather jacket and stood anxious to try it on.

"Whew." Lou seemed very relieved.

"You thought I wouldn't like it?"

"It's not exactly your style. I was hoping it might make you feel a little more comfortable when you meet everyone."

"Won't these girls be mad I have their patch when they've never even met me?" I untied my robe and dropped it to the floor carelessly.

"I asked Liz about that, she said she would give them a heads up. They refer to themselves as Sisters, like we call each other Bro, or brother. I'm not too clear on the details, you'll have to ask Liz when we get there, but she said the patch is to identify you as one of our old ladies. I think you're good babe." He assured me. "She would have told me otherwise. I know women can be catty, but not Liz. She is the wife of my club's president, if she says it's ok, it is."

"I still feel weird wearing it." I shrugged it on my shoulders. "It fits perfect!"

"Good. That was another concern. I had to sneak a peek at your wardrobe for the size." He confessed.

I caught another patch on the front and looked at it closer. "What does the bear mean?" There's a little brown bear sewn into the leather above my left breast.

Lou leaned forward pulling me closer. He studied the patch and rolled his eyes. "Termite's idea of a joke. Bear used to be my nickname. I never liked it, so everyone calls me Lou, if they don't want a fist in the face."

"Why Bear?" I asked as he pulled me to sit on his lap.

He exhaled, "When I was prospecting I kept rejecting all their nicknames. The guys were getting pissed at me. Anyway, we got a call to the shop one day that a bear had gotten into some lady's minivan and they needed help getting it out. We didn't have local game and fish services back then. At least none that were close by."

"Anyway, I rode out with the tow truck since we were sure the van would be destroyed. I don't know what came over me, but when we got to the park I started barking orders sending people to their cars, or as far away as possible. The park service was just standing around waiting for animal control.

"I watched the bear get more and more agitated and started feeling sorry for it. I made sure everyone was safe then walked over and slid the door open. I stood back against the passenger door hoping he'd bolt.

"He hopped out of the van then turned right to me. I about shit myself when the bear went up on it's hind legs. Termite told me afterwards the bear waved it's paws in the air and turned to trot off into the woods. He says the bear looked like he was thanking me. I had my eyes closed bracing for an attack, so I didn't see. Afterwards I found out the guys all had their guns out and ready to shoot. I'm glad they didn't have to."

"Lou, you could have been killed!! Why would you put yourself in that kind of danger??"

"I was young and dumb baby. Anyway, they called me Bear after that. I put up with it until I became a member, then I put an end to it, or tried to."

"Why? I like Bear. You're cuddly and safe like a big soft teddy bear. Not only that but you make a living keeping people safe. It fits."

"Bears don't protect people."

"No, maybe not, but a big soft teddy bear always makes a girl feel safe." I snuggled into him burying my nose in his neck and playing with his beard again. It's getting so long.

"Don't get any ideas about calling me Bear." He warned me.

"I would never call you anything you didn't like." I promised.

He stood taking me with him. "Ready for bed?"

"Please." I begged. "Are you coming?"

"I still need a shower my love, then yes." He walked me to the large bed and tucked me between the sheets after helping me out of my jacket.

I was asleep before my head it the pillow.

For the first time in two weeks *I* was able to sleep in as late as I wanted. Which wasn't too late since there is once again a very large biker nuzzling me in his sleep. I'm learning to tell by his breathing when he's really asleep, and when he's faking it. He tries to fake his breathing, but I'm wise to his games now.

This is Lou asleep. He smells so good. Not just hotel soap, but his special Lou-only scent. I can smell it past the shampoo and body wash. I inhale deeply taking in all I can, waking him. Lou is a very light sleeper.

He kissed my neck as he woke, "Good morning my love."

I hugged him to me. "Good morning."

"I have something for you." He lifted some of his weight off my upper body making what is now pressed into my thigh very evident.

I smiled and tried to moved his hair out of his eyes. It's not cooperating, but it's fun to play with. "I bet you do."

"How did you sleep?" He nosed the spaghetti strap of my blue nightgown down over my shoulder.

"Very well, and you?"

"I sleep too well with you." He kissed his way down moving the fabric with his beard until he found a nipple to suckle.

"Good." What are we talking about again?

He raked his fingers over my breasts taking the gown with him as I lift up for his mouth. He filled his hands and squeezed gently kneading as he suckled one, then the other. The tingling that's building from my core is spreading to my limbs. I find myself wanting more. More touching, more kissing, more flesh.

I can't reach him like this, but I think that's on purpose. When his kisses and skillful finger moved further down I knew I was in trouble. He slid my robe down off my hips and ankles.

"You are one beautiful woman Barbara. The most beautiful I've ever seen. You should be on the covers of magazines, but I'm going to selfishly keep all this to myself." He put his hands between my knees and pushed them apart. "Don't be shy."

I covered my face with my hands and wondered how I'd survive his looking at me like this!!

His finger found me eager for him once more. "You are so sweet. Do you know what it does to man's ego to find a woman so wet for him?"

"I think have an idea."

"Yeah, you got me good on that one. Maybe it's time for a little payback. I've been gentle with you so far, but you're a bad girl for letting me come in your mouth after I told you not to." He pushed that finger into me making me yelp a little. "Maybe we'll see how you like it a little harder and faster this time."

His playful threats should not have been taken so lightly. He added a second finger and sped up, landing deep and almost pulling completely free with each powerful stroke. My body wants more and my hips push towards him for me.

"Shit honey. Oh man. Come for me. Please. Do it now Barbara, let go. Oh shit." He bit my knee as I came making it all that much sweeter.

All too quickly he pulled free and got up on his knees between my legs. Before I could panic he was pouring himself onto my stomach as he falls forward to capture my left nipple and suckle al title to hard. I moaned in pleasure and pain as he repeated the same thing on the other side.

"Ow, easy Lou." I begged softly not wanting to alarm him and deter from his obvious release.

He set his forehead on my chest trying to catch his breath. "Wow."

"I couldn't have said it better."

He sat back, "Don't move, I'll be right back."

"Okay. I don't think I could move if I wanted to."

"Holy hell." He stumbled into the dresser. "Ow, fuck." He hopped on one foot for a couple steps making me giggle.

"Are you alright??"

"I don't even know my name right now." He disappeared into the bathroom and came back out with a wet towel and a dry one.

I watched as he cleaned off my stomach. "Thank you."

"For what? Making a mess all over you like some teenage boy with no control?" He's not too happy with himself.

"Actually, yes." I waited until he look at me like I was nuts before continuing, "Yes. It's nice to know I'm not the only one with control issues." I took his hand pulling him back onto the bed with me.

He dropped the towels to the floor and pulled the sheet over us as he settled down alongside me. "I should be better, for you."

I hugged his head to my shoulder as he wrapped around me, "I love you. You are better for me. You brought light into my life. Even with everything that's going on you've found a way to make me feel safe and loved. On top of that you show me all these wonderful things in bed, and dressing rooms." I teased kissing the top of his head.

"I love you too, but I need to find more control with you."

"Why? So you can take away that wonderful feeling I get when you look like that? No way. I hear it's good for the skin, so feel free to do that again." I can't believe I said that.

Neither could he because his head came up and the look of shock made me laugh a little too hard. He tickled me with sweet threats of exactly where he was going to it next.

Once he got me pinned and breathless he smiled slyly down at me, "So I guess staying in bed and making love all day is out?"

I laughed and tried again to buck him off. "Yes! I need coffee before I can function." He let me escape this time and followed me to the bathroom. He stopped just behind me in the mirror.

I looked at him as I loaded my toothbrush. "What?"

"I like the way we look together. We fit." He said simply.

Once again he's caught me off guard, "We do?"

He pointed to the mirror, "Look. You don't see it?"

I looked, "All I see is you." With him in the picture all I want to do is look at him. I turned around and looked up. "Do you really want to get married??"

"Of course I do. Why do ask?"

"I was thinking, or maybe dreaming since I was so tired last evening."

"Thinking about what sweetheart?" He stepped back and sat on the side of the large tub.

"Well, I want Myles to give me away for one thing, but the other is a little harder to say."

"I'm not going to bite you for telling me how you feel. I want Myles to give you away too. What else?"

I fidgeted a little, "I want to meet your family first, before we, you know, sleep together all the way. I need to know they'll accept me. I know you gave me the jacket, but I need to know they like me."

"Of course they'll like you. I love you, they will too." He assured me.

"There's a saying in the south that when you marry a person you also marry their family. I've seen plenty of cases where families didn't like each other and it tore the couples apart."

"Movies?" He teased.

I relaxed because he's not mad like I thought he might be. "And books!!"

His eyes are bright and playful, "Relax love. I'm not going to rush you into anything. We have a long ride tomorrow before I can get you home and tucked into my bed. The following day I have to work, so you'll meet Liz and the rest of the crew. Women are women, aside from Liz, you might get that typical skeptical welcome at first.

Once they spend five minutes with you they'll see what I see and fall head over heels just like I have."

"You're quite the silver-tongued devil, you know that?"

"If you say so. Liz will welcome you with open arms, that's just who she is."

"Who is Liz?, all you said was she's your club's president's wife." I turned to pick up my toothbrush and brush while he talks.

"Liz is The General's wife. The chapter I belong to is called General's Tribe. It was started on an old Indian reserve back in the day and because the guy who started it is a retired Army General, it became General's Tribe. When I told her I was in love with you she about blew my eardrum screaming in delight."

I finished brushing and rinsed before turning back to him. "She sounds very nice."

"She's a wonderful person, you'll like her. She's also a viper when it comes to protecting her family. I've seen that woman go off, and it ain't pretty."

"Ain't is not a word Lou." I teased him.

"I used it for emphasis Miss Whitmore. Are you going to smack my hand with a ruler? Or wash my mouth out with soap?"

I laughed feeling the weight lift from my shoulders. "Are you going to get out of here so I can get dressed?"

He stood up and flipped up the lid on the toilet, "I gotta pee first."

I covered my face with my hands, "LOU!!! You could have asked me for some privacy!"

"Why? What's the big deal? Couples pee in front of each other all the time." He smiled at me enjoying my torment!

"The big deal is I don't tinkle in front of people!!" I had to laugh though.

"Tinkle?? Now that's too cute." He teased flushing then washing his hands.

That's when I knew it was safe to come out from hiding and peeked, "You sir, have zero manners."

He smiled, like one happy man, at me through the mirror, "You can spend the rest of your life trying to teach me."

I felt my eyes roll and my cheeks puff up as I smiled even bigger. Lou is turning out to be quite fun. I could get used to this. This not being alone. I pushed the thought away of just how totally alone I've been my entire life, except for Myles.

"You okay sweetheart?" He's drying his hands and turned to look at me now.

I shook off the thoughts, "Yes. I just got lost in thought for a second."

"About what?" He's interested. Truly interested. Wow. This man. This big, wonderful, powerful biker of a man cares about what *I'm* thinking.

"Myles has been my lifetime companion and protector. I never felt alone because of him, but now that you're here, I realize just how lonely I was." I motioned to us and the bathroom, "The way we can talk, and joke with each other. I had no idea, it's a bit unsettling to see all that I've been missing in life."

"Me too. I like it very much. So much I want it every day for the rest of my life." He walked over and kissed me softly, "I'm going to order coffee and breakfast. Any preferences for breakfast?"

"Just the pleasure of your company."

"Always." He kissed me again then left after touching my chin and giving me one last loving look.

9

"What are we going to do today? Besides the rings of course, which I think can wait." I hinted.

"No waiting. I want an engagement ring on your finger now." He pointed to my hand from across the table. We're having an elaborate breakfast of omelets, pancakes, bacon, sausage, pastries, and fruit.

"Did you talk to your bug friend about lunch?"

He almost choked on his mouthful of bacon before managing, "My bug friend?"

"Termite?"

"Oh! No, I'll call him in a little while. That bug doesn't do mornings. We'll be lucky if he makes it out for lunch. Knowing Mary she'll drag him out anxious to meet you." He added.

"How did he get his nickname?"

"They made him eat termites when he was prospecting. He developed a taste for them and began eating them all around the club. Chocolate covered, salted, roasted with cayenne pepper, you name it."

"That is disgusting."

"I agree, but he still eats the damn things."

"Let's hope not for lunch today."

"No, he usually refrains in restaurants. Aside from touring the old penitentiary, there're a few museums, a bird of prey park, a zoo, and a botanical garden we can explore today if you would like." He sat back finally full. He eats a large amount of food. Then again, he's a large man.

"I get the feeling museums would bore you to pieces, and I have no interest in exploring a prison, new or old. I vote for the birds of prey and the botanical garden. That way you get something manly, and I get more flowers." I sat back picking up my coffee.

"Today isn't about me, it's about you. I want to spoil you."

"No, you said we should get to know each other. Each other. That means both of us. Do you like the birds of prey idea, or not?"

He shrugged, "Sounds interesting enough."

"I thought so too." An idea hit me. "What's your favorite color?"

He tilted his head, "I don't think I have one, why?"

"Not even black?"

He laughed, "Maybe, if I had to pick one. Why are you asking me this?"

"To get to know you better. Favorite song?"

He shook his head, "I got nothing. The only 'favorite' I have, is you."

"That's silly. You have to have likes and dislikes." I argued playfully, and horribly curious all of a sudden.

"I like you. I dislike being away from you."

"Lou, you're being difficult again. Just tell me. I want to know the man I'm going to marry, if all goes well that is." I added and instantly regretted it as the look on his face changed to one I hope to never see again.

"Please don't do that."

"I'm sorry, it came out wrong. I love you. I want to marry you, but I worry. I worry that being with me is putting you and your family in danger."

"I know that, but you're safer with me than without me. Are you trying to give me another 'out' Miss Whitmore?" He asked suspiciously.

"I don't want you to think you have to marry me for me to sleep with you."

He let out an exasperated breath and slapped his napkin on the table. He shook his head and looked up at me. "Do you really think I need to marry you to get you into bed? Do I look that desperate?"

"Desperate? No." I'm confused.

"If I wanted you just for the sex, that part would have been over and done with and I'd be on to my next job. Think about it Barbara."

"I'm sorry. I guess I'm not very good at this."

"Just try to trust me. This isn't about getting laid. Not to sound like an ass, but I can get that anywhere I want."

"Yeah, I remember."

"Geezus. I thought you'd let that go? I did that because I don't fuck every woman in my path and I was pent up to the point of it being painful. If I had known it was going to be thrown in my face by the woman I love I never would have done it." He started to stand.

I panicked, "Lou, wait. I'm sorry. Really, please, don't leave."

"Leave?" He looked at me with his hands on the back of the chair, "Who said I was leaving?"

"I . . . you got up." I feel stupid all over.

"I'm not going anywhere that easily, but nice try. My favorite bike is the Road King, I prefer side roads to open freeways, and I like strong dark beers. I like my job because it gives me purpose. And I fucking love you with every fiber of my being. I would appreciate it if you would start believing that."

"I'm trying." I stood and went to him. "I'm sorry. Forgive me?"

"Always." He cupped my butt and pulled me against him. "You have a spa appointment in ten minutes. Think that's enough time for dessert?" He kissed my neck making me relax and melt into his arms.

"Not for both of us." I pushed him back. "Sit."

"Oh no. You got away with that once."

"And I'll get away with it anytime I damn well please. Sit." I smacked his butt and pulled the chair back.

"Babe, seriously." He sat when I pushed the spot on his hip that makes the legs weak. I pushed his a little harder than you're supposed to, so he sent down quickly. "Whoa. What was that?"

"Pressure points. I learned them in self defense class." I decided to get his jeans completely out of my way before beginning play time.

"Barbara!! Shit!!!" I was five minutes late for my mani-pedi. The image of Lou sated and shocked still sitting in that chair as I left, lingered with me the entire two hours.

"It's too big. I'll run my hose."

"Hose? Pantyhose?" He leaned into my ear to whisper, "No more pantyhose, those things are stifling and get in my way. Besides, you have the softest, sexiest legs on earth. Why would you want to cover them up?"

I took the large emerald engagement ring off and handed it back to the jewelry sales person. "Do you have something smaller? The hose keep my legs warm, and I wear a lot of dresses, or used to until I met you. Seattle is chilly from what I understand." I explained.

He groaned low in his throat making me laugh.

"I told you I have simple taste in jewelry." I said as the salesman brought over another tray.

"These are typically anniversary rings, but they seem to be to more to the lady's liking." He said looking at me. I get the feeling he's intimidated by the large leather clad biker standing next to me.

I'd taken my jacket off on the way inside the store, Lou keeps his on almost constantly no matter where he is, unless we're inside, and alone.

I played with the rings and found one emerald band, and a matching diamond band. I lifted my hand to admire them. "That's better."

Lou looked them over and smirked, "You deserve something much bigger."

"If you buy me some giant rock I won't wear it every day. You do want me to have something I can wear every day, right?" I challenged him.

"Yes, you know I do." He picked up the box with his the ring it and handed it to the guy behind the counter. "Here, we'll take these." He pulled out his wallet and gave him a credit card. "I'm going to go get some air."

I grabbed his sleeve before he could turn away, "Hey. Are you mad?"

He touched my cheek, "No, just stubborn. I wanted to put a rock on your finger for my own selfish reasons."

"Which are?"

He glanced over at the salesman, "Not to be discussed here. I'm going to go call my bug friend and see about a late lunch." He kissed my cheek and went outside.

I turned back to the counter and picked up his ring. When the guy came back over I pulled the ring from it's box and showed it to him. "How long would it take to engrave this?"

"A few minutes. It's free with your purchase. What would you like it to say?" He picked up a pen and paper to write.

I looked over my shoulder to make sure Lou is still outside. "I would like it to say, 'My life began with you. Forever Yours, Barbie.'" Okay so it's a little corny, but it made me tear up just thinking about the smile on his face when he reads that at our wedding.

We made a couple adjustments to the font just in time as Lou found his way back inside.

"All set?" He asked sounding much happier now.

"What did you do? Take a happy pill?" I just need to stall him for a few minutes.

"No. I talked to Liz. She told me to tell you Myles had your things shipped to her house. We can pick them up anytime. Your phone, laptop, and whatever else was in your purse."

"Not the purse? I don't really care, but what did they do? Dump my things out of my purse into a shipping box?"

He smiled wickedly, "She said you'd ask about the purse, and told me to ask, 'What purse?' I think that means she swiped it, but don't worry, I'm sure she's kidding."

I laughed making sure I kept Lou's attention while Robert went into the back to make the engraving on Lou's ring. "She can have the purse, I have a new one." I reached up and tugged on his beard gently. "I think I'm getting used to this. It's much softer now."

He saw right through me, "What are you up to?"

I tried to hide the smile, but I'm no good at surprises, therefore I failed miserably. "Nothing for you to concern yourself about."

He looked around, "Where's Robert?"

"I suppose he's cleaning the rings."

"Didn't he do that ten times showing them to us?"

"Impatient are we?"

"To marry you? Yes."

"Did you talk to Termite?" I changed the subject not ready to discus wedding plans just yet. The rings are enough for one day.

He smiled and visibly relaxed a little, "Yes. He's going to meet us at the usual haunt. You'll get to meet some friends of mine outside the club. They call themselves HOGs. It stands for Harley Owners Group."

He reached for the bag but I snatched it away. "I'll be holding these thank you." I waited while Lou signed the receipt before snatching that too. I wasn't sure if Robert had written anything about the engraving on it.

"Afraid I'll loose them?, or back out?" He accused, then Lou thanked Robert and escorted me from the building.

"No. You can't back out, you just spent a fortune on the rings, and this way I can peek at them, it's a girl thing " I teased him as I hugged him around the waist with my right arm while we walked over to his bike. "Plus you don't need to be in charge of everything, especially something so delicate."

"I'm in charge of you, and you're much more delicate." He argued.

"You're in charge of protecting me, not in charge of my actions." I countered enjoying this more playful bickering than the bickering we did when we first met.

"I beg to differ." He hinted as he opened the saddlebag for me to put my purse inside. We've developed a sort of routine now when it comes to mounting and un-mounting this bike.

"You do huh?"

"Well, yes." He grabbed me around the waist and set my tush on his seat before pulling my legs up around his waist. He used those big capable hands to secure me in place before kissing my socks off.

When he finally slowed and lifted up I was breathless and left wanting more. His eyes flickered across mine, "Tell me again I have no control over your actions." He dared me.

I gave him a look a mother gives a child trying to get away with something, "You cheat Mr. Colson."

He smiled that boyish confident smile I like so much better than Grumpy Lou. "For you my love, I would cheat, lie, steal, kill, and anything else I needed to do to get your lovely sweet lips on mine."

"I love you too."

When he parked us among a sea of bikes outside what appeared to be a biker bar, I gripped his shirt under his cut. "We're going in there??" I asked as Lou turned the engine off.

"It's just a bar Barbie. Do you really think I'd take you somewhere unsafe?" He asked helping me off the bike before he pulls himself off to stand and take my helmet.

"You're right. I have you, I shouldn't be worried."

He draped his arm over my shoulders and led me to the door. "Termite said everyone here today is meeting to plan the charity runs for the year. The HOGs meet up for beers with some of the local chapters and clubs to arrange starting, and stopping points, raffle arrangements, which charities go with which runs. Shit like that."

"So we're walking in on a benefit meeting?" I looked up as he opened the door for me.

"Pretty much, yes."

"Huh." This is the last thing I expected. I stepped inside and looked around. It's not quite as nice as Red's bar in Arizona, but it seems welcoming somehow. Like a big leather living room where you can spill food and drinks without worrying about it. "Why do they call it Cricket's?"

"Who knows. I've only been in here a few times, usually I party at the club where I can drink and stumble to my bike and pass out in the parking lot."

"What??" I stopped before we got to the table with what I'm assuming are the couple we're supposed to meet.

He looked down, "What?"

"You sleep in parking lots??"

"Not public ones, at the clubhouses. I put down a blanket first . . . usually." He seems so amused, I relaxed.

"How did you manage to keep from getting run over?"

"We bikers all drink together, so none of us can ride at the same time."

"You do??"

He laughed, "No honey. Come on, let me introduce you to one crazy old man, and his wife who deserves better."

"No more teasing me. This is difficult enough." I scolded him.

"Yes my love." He said obediently, even though there is not an obedient bone in that man's body. He ushered me over to to the table and looked at the couple who stood to shake our hands, "Termite, this is my soon to be wife, Barbara. Barbie, this is Mary, that crazy bastard's old lady." He said cheerfully.

Termite kissed the back of my hand, hazels eyes full of innocent mischief, "Miss Barbara, it's a pleasure to meet the woman who lassoed this big oaf in."

Mary shook my hand next drawing my attention away from her husband, "Nice to meet you. How do you like the jacket??" She has a warm smile. I like her right away.

I turned around, "I love it! Thank you!"

She clapped, "Yeah!! Beer?" She asked as I sat next to Lou.

"Yes, please."

Lou pulled my chair closer resting his arm around behind me. "What's new with you two trouble makers?"

Termite sat back looking back and forth between us. I wonder if Lou's beard will get that long. "Not much, Mary's sister is getting married in a couple weeks, so my house is filling up with giddy women." He pretended to complain then leaned across the table to Lou, "Help. Take me with you. Please. I'll pay you a million dollars cash."

I laughed out loud earning an appreciative laugh in return from Mary. "How long are you two in town for?"

Lou replied before I could. "Just tonight. Liz is anxious to meet Barbie. If I don't get her home in time for the poker run and rally this weekend, she'll skin me alive."

"I wish we could come up, but it's a little too far with all these wedding plans. With me still working full time, the weekends are the only time we get anything done."

"What kind of work do you do?"

"I'm a social worker. I help abused kids for the most part. I love my job. Termite wants me to quit, but I can't bring myself to let go." She confided like we've known each other for years.

For the next four hours we talked more than drank. Lou switched to water after two beers. I nursed four beers. I figured one an hour wouldn't hurt, and I'm not driving.

By the time we left I felt like I was saying goodbye to old friends. I even found myself inviting them to a wedding I was not entirely sure was going to happen.

Lou looked uncomfortable when Mary asked where my ring was. I told her we'd just purchased them and I wanted to wait to reveal them later. She took the hint and left it at that with a warm hug goodbye. First Georgia, then Red, now Mary. I Have FRIENDS!! That may seem silly to most, but for me it's a huge step outside of my simple, boring little world.

I did a silly little twirl in the middle of the fancy hotel room when we got back. "That was fun!"

Lou set his cut on the chair as he walked towards me with a very seductive look in his eyes.

It gave me butterflies and stopped me in my tracks. "You look like you're hunting."

"Maybe I am." He hinted.

I put my hand to my stomach, "When you look at me like that I get full of gitters."

"I don't know what gitters are, but I'd like to kiss them."

I bumped into the wall. "Oh."

"Stop moving Barbara."

"I'm trying."

He caught up to me and tucked my hair behind my ear, "I want to kiss you, and kiss only you, for the rest of my life."

"Oh!" I barely got that out before he closed in and kissed me until the next thing I know I'm on my back under him on the bed. I found myself nervous he might take this too far.

It took me a little while, but it finally became clear all he wanted was exactly what he'd said he wanted. I let myself go and relaxed finding his kiss to be much more intimate than I thought possible. It's like we can communicate with the slightest, or deepest, touch of our tongues.

I gently pulled on his earlobes to stop him.

He lifted up slowly and smiled down at me, "Hi."

I felt myself squirm under his weight. "We should get some sleep. We have a long ride ahead tomorrow."

"We haven't eaten."

"I ate a ton of fries this afternoon, but if you're hungry . . ." I had been too caught up in his kisses to think about food.

"I'm going to order some dinner. You go get ready for me to kiss you to sleep." He helped me up reminding me we're both still fully dressed.

"Good idea."

10

─❦─

I looked at his big beautiful bike and rubbed my rump. "I might be reaching my limit."

Lou kneaded the other cheek, "I'll give them a good fluffing when we get home."

"I want to buy a camera before we get too far. It gets boring back there." I'm glad I remembered before we got started.

"Boring eh?" He's working those bungee cords like a Chinese puzzle.

"Well, you get to focus on driving, and I get to stare at your vicious patch. Not that it's not beautiful, in a dark manly sort of way, but other than the scenery, it's pretty boring."

He laughed, "Feel free to let you hands wander. I'll stop you if it gets too distracting. We'll get you a camera in a couple stops, none of the electronics stores are open."

"A disposable will be fine."

"We'll start with that, but you deserve better." He kissed my cheek before straddling and righting his big bike. It amazes me how he can hold the beast upright. Although he does have some rather strong limbs. And those abs. "Barbara?"

"Yes?" I blinked trying to focus.

"Where'd you go baby?"

"I'm not telling you." I laughed and took his hand to climb on behind him. I've come to love it here. It's become my favorite place in the world, with the exception of being in his arms at night.

I ran into the drug store to buy two disposable cameras, and came out with a book, two cameras, some hard candy, and a handful of cards to send notes to my new friends. Lou can get me the addresses later.

We stopped to buy a good camera a little over an hour later, then again for lunch shortly after noon.

"What's that?" He nodded towards my cards on the table.

"I wanted to write some thank you notes to my new friends. Being on the road all the time hasn't left me much room for phone calls. Can you get me some addresses?"

"Sure. That's very nice of you. I don't think I've seen someone write a thank you card since I was five."

I smiled and set the pen down to give him my full attention. "I've always written them to strangers for donations and assistance with events, so it's nice to write to people I feel like I know for a change."

"Bet you didn't see this coming a couple weeks ago?" He took a big bite of pancake.

"No, admittedly, I did not foresee falling in love with a big bratty biker and his entire family." I teased him as I nibbled on the rest of the fruit on my plate.

He raised an eyebrow at me, "I'm bratty?"

"Well, maybe bratty is a little harsh."

He sat back looking at me. "You're beautiful with your hair down. The leather and tight jeans are a nice touch too. You really are beautiful Barbara. No matter what you're wearing, but I like this look the best."

I felt myself blush, "I like this look the best too. Although you are not going to keep me from my stilettos. I can still wear those with jeans."

"I look forward to it. I suppose we should arrange to have your things shipped across country."

"I'll take care of that. There will be plenty of correspondence back and forth as I figure out what to do with the plantation. Dad . . . Mr. Whitmore was offered decent money for the land a couple times over the years. I'm sure if I put it up for sale and divvy up the profits, I can afford to give everyone some kind of severance package."

"Let Myles take care of it."

"Myles and I will be taking care of it. Hopefully neither of will need to go back for any reason."

"You're not going back there period. It's too dangerous." He informed me.

"We'll cross that bridge when we get there. If we get there."

"Uh, no. Bridge crossed babe. You are NOT going back to that, plantation. Seriously, can we call it something else?"

I laughed, "Call it 'the house' then. I don't want to fight about what-if's." I picked up the pen to finish the one I'd started to Red.

"Let's get out of here so I can kiss that polite little mouth of yours." He waved the waitress over.

I can't help but smile and absently touched my lip before moving it to hold the card as I wrote.

"Barbie?"

"Don't call me that."

"Barbie Barbie Barbie." He teased just as a small chunk of ice landed between my breasts.

"Lou!" I frantically dug it out and threw it back at his smug face. It wasn't much more than a flick of water by the time I got that far, but the effort was apparent, and he still ducked.

His laugh is infectious. I put the cards back in my purse as he paid the bill. On the way to the bike in the parking lot he asked, "How's the photography going back there?"

"Good. It took a few minutes to figure it all out, but I think I've got it now."

"When we get back on the freeway hand it to me and look over my shoulder. I'll take a couple pictures of us."

"You should keep both hands (his look stopped me) . . . you're right. Never mind."

"I can ride with no hands babe, I just don't because that would be stupid with you on the back. I can do one hand, watch the road, and take a few pictures. It might take a few to get one that's centered right, but you have the big memory card. You can afford the space."

"I didn't mean to question your riding skills."

"It's not just that. I want you to trust me. When you say you love me, then you don't trust me, it's a little irritating." He handed me my helmet.

"I'm sorry. That was not my intention." I put my hand on his arm, "Lou. Please don't be mad."

He leaned in and kissed my cheek, "I'm not mad baby. Trust takes time to build, I'm just impatient."

"You are not. You've been most patient with me, about everything. I don't know if I told you this, but I am sorry for snapping at you back in Vegas. I never wanted you to leave. I don't know why I said that to you."

He pulled me in for a hug. "Oh honey, you don't have to apologize. You were mad, and fired up. I understand completely."

I hugged him back, and it felt so good. Every time I touch this man I feel at home. This is a new feeling, the only thing close was when I was in school.

He kissed the top of my head, "Hey. You okay?"

I leaned back and looked up, "Better than I've ever been. When you hold me I feel like I finally belong somewhere. Then we get on this bike and I feel so free at the same time. Like nothing can touch us. Nothing can catch us. Part of me wants to keep going forever."

He cupped my face, "We will keep going forever, together. Anywhere you want to go, I'll take you, and anytime you want to go home, you come right here." He pulled me in for a long sweet hug.

We stopped a couple hours later to stretch and take pictures. The ones Lou took while we were riding came out a lot better than I expected they would. I'm trying to flip through the images on the camera before we resume our trip, but Mr. Wandering hands is distracting me.

"Lou, stop that. People can see."

"That's why I turned you around. All they see is my back." He tickled my neck with that beard as he kissed. He breathed out a little too hard in my ear making me squeal and laugh as goosebumps consumed my flesh.

"Lou!! Behave yourself!" I almost dropped the camera when his hand slid all too easily right down the front of my jeans. I stilled as he quickly got my attention under my panties. "Oh my. Not here."

"Shh. Nobody can see. Let go a little Barbie. I want to show you something."

"Here??"

He laughed, "Not that silly, and of course not here. You are so adorably innocent." He pushed into me and my innocence shattered. "That a girl. Trust me." His words cut me to the quick. They also inflamed my desire to both please him, and let go to see what only he can show me.

I leaned back against him and tilted my head so he could get at my neck easier. He took it as a sign of my surrender, which it very much was, and tightened his grip as he brought me faster and harder to a climax that rocked me to my southern roots.

"Oh my. Don't let go." I begged.

"Never. I will never let go of you my love. Put your helmet on. I want you to feel this bike between your sensitive legs."

"What???" I about fell into the bike.

He caught my arm and laughed. "You'll see."

"I probably don't want to know."

"Oh, you want to know. Trust me. You *need* to know." He assured me with a wicked gleam in his eyes.

I put my forehead between his shoulder blades and cussed him inside my head.

I can feel him shaking with laughter so I smacked his arm. "You could have warned me!!!"

He can't stop laughing. I'm not sure if I came, maybe I did, it was a little tough to tell with all the vibration. Maybe it was just that he brought it to my attention, or maybe it was just being sensitive down there after what he'd done, but he was horribly right.

Finally the assault on my lower body ceased and I could think straight again. I leaned forward so he leaned back a little. "You're mean!!"

He turned and kissed me quickly. "Bored back there now baby??"

I sat back, "No, definitely not bored." Oh my. Who am I?? All these new people and experiences are clouding over my old life, which feels like a really long boring movie I've been sitting through.

Since the day Lou came into my life I've had the wind in my hair, been shot at, tickled, kissed, made friends, and oh yeah. Lou's . . . body. Just thinking about his body is making me all too aware of the large thunderous engine between my legs. The bike isn't helping either. The joke in my head made me smile.

"You know I can see you, right??" He asked over his shoulder.

I leaned in and kissed his cheek. "You see me alright." I'm not sure if he heard that, but he brought my arms around to hug him tightly. I held him for a while until sunrise pictures beckoned.

We stopped again at a grocery store. "Almost there babe. I haven't been home for a while so the house is empty."

"I'm grateful for the chance to walk around a bit. Do you shop here regularly when you're home?"

"I do. You should get used to saying that."

"Saying what?"

"I do."

"I do, what?" I'm confused. Maybe I'm tired.

He stopped when we reached the sidewalk and turned to lift my chin, "Yup, you're tired. I think eight hours is your limit babe. Just hold onto me, I'll do the shopping, unless you see something you want, then just throw it in the basket of course."

"I look that tired?"

"You look a little road weary, but you're doing great. I'm so proud of you I could burst. Two weeks ago you were a stuffy little southern belle. Now you're my beautiful southern biker babe. You amaze me at every turn, I told you that. Loving you is like watching a big beautiful flower bloom every day."

I'm lost in bright blue eyes and soft sweet words. Myles has complimented me before, on my clothing, grades, or achievements, but Lou's kind words are completely different. "Thank you. I've been a little nervous during this transition."

"I bet you have." He smiled and kissed me before leading me inside. "You've been very brave. What would you like for dinner?"

"A pillow and a massage." I leaned into him and rubbed my tush.

"I can help you with both of those once we get home." He assured me.

"And a hot bath?" I looked up hopeful he has hot water and a bathtub.

"Yes, I have a very nice tub with your name on it."

We picked out the basics to get us through a couple days. I offered to carry the bags, but Lou worked his bungee ninja magic and managed to secure everything on his bike. He definitely knows his bike. I was certain nothing else could fit on that bike, but he proved me wrong.

11

Ten minutes later he pulled up in front of a rather large mansion, I assume, to visit a friend, "What are we doing here?"

"Hopefully a lot of sex, and maybe raising some kids. If you want kids. I could go either way." He dug around in his saddle bag and pulled out a remote. The garage door opened and he walked the bike right inside like he owned the place.

Then his words hit me. "Wait . . . what?? This . . . this is your house???"

He smiled and did that mischievous eyebrow dance again. "Our house. Welcome home love." He grabbed my bag and one of his before holding a door open for me. "In you go."

I all but ran inside. I feel like I'm seeing into his soul.

He flipped on the lights as the house unfolded in front of me. "Lou, this is amazing."

"I had a little help, but designed most of it myself. Contractors did the electrical and drywall. I had a hand in, or did a good bit of, the rest. Unfortunately I have no clue what to put in here. I can build shit, but I can't stock it." He set our bags down by a sleeping bag that was in the middle of the living room floor.

I walked over to the wall of windows, "Honey, this view is incredible!" There's a lake lined with boats, and the city below is lighting up as the sky darkens above. It's dark, but beautiful.

"I'm glad you approve." He came up and wrapped his arms around me. "Think you can be happy here?"

"Are you kidding me??" I turned around. "I can't believe you let me think you lived in some average house in town or something. I would have been happy there too, but this is incredible! And why didn't you tell me??"

He shrugged, "I like surprising you, your face lights up. I wanted to see that look on you face again, like when you opened the present from the girls."

"You must make some pretty good money being a transporter, or whatever you call it."

"Sometimes. I'm also an architect."

"What??" I leaned back, "You are??"

"I didn't tell you?"

"NO!! You said you were a transporter, someone who takes people to safety."

"Oh, well, that's what I was for you. I'm sorry, I guess it hasn't come up. I take a few contracts a year and work on them between jobs for the club, and some on the road. The only room in this house that's half furnished is my office. I needed some tools, drafting table, desk, storage for drafts, stuff like that." He took my hand, "Let's go get our things so you can get in that bath, and I can get you naked."

"Oh Lou, I don't know if I have the energy for all that tonight." I whined as he drew me back through the beautiful house with it's vaulted ceilings, are those antique wood beams?, stone fireplace, and wrought iron light fixtures.

"For your massage Barbie, get your mind out of the gutter."

I laughed as he handed me bags, "It's your fault. You've corrupted my mind and my mouth. I keep catching myself cussing."

"I'd like to corrupt your mouth some more." He teased and stole a kiss from lips as he held the door for me with hands full of bags too.

"You're terrible."

"You'll have to teach me some manners." He followed me to the kitchen where we dropped our bags.

He picked up the ones with our clothes, "Follow me."

"What about these?"

"I'll take care of those. You need a soak. Then we'll eat, and start on your massage. You've been a trooper the last couple days. I want to spoil you."

Lou's bathroom is incredible. High ceilings with skylights so clear you can see the stars. He'd brought me a beer from the six-pack we'd bought earlier and vowed to leave me to my nice long hot bath.

So when he opened the door and stood in the doorway with the ring box in his hand I sat up. "You snooped."

"I unpacked." He corrected and walked over to kneel beside the tub. "I . . . don't know what to say. Thank you."

"You're not supposed to thank me nosy." I teased and splashed his ever growing beard with bubbles.

He took my ring from the box and picked up my left hand. "Will you marry me Barbara? Will you be my wife?"

My heart is pounding in my chest. Up until this moment I haven't taken his talk of marriage seriously. Even after buying the rings it didn't feel real. "Lou, I . . ." And that's when I saw it.

He looked up at me with those crystal light blue eyes and I knew there was no way I could say no. There's a fear in those eyes that breaks my heart.

"Yes. I will be your wife." He caught me off guard, but there was only one answer.

He exhaled and slid the ring on my finger. "I've never been so relieved in my life. I thought you were going to say no for a second there."

"Saying yes came so easily it knocked me off balance, plus you surprised me."

He leaned in and kissed me until he fell into the tub with me. Water went everywhere, but we didn't notice until I shivered, what was left of the water had cooled around us.

We took a quick hot shower and dressed for bed. He in his boxers, and me in my sweats. I'm chilly, he seems to be comfortable.

I slid the sleeping bag over by the window while he gathered dinner from the kitchen, "Aren't you cold?"

"I need to be a little cold right now babe. Are you? I can turn up the heat."

"I'm okay, but I'm wearing quite a bit more."

He sat down putting plates of fried chicken and macaroni salad in front of us. "Showering with you like that will take me a little while to recover from." He picked up my hand. "You're chilly. Hang on." He looked up. "Computer on."

A voice from the sky, not unlike Turner's Daisy, replied, "Welcome home sir. What can I do for you?"

"Put some heat to the floors for me, seventy-six should do it."

"Yes sir. Shall I add your guest to the system?"

"Yes. Her name is Barbara Whitmore, soon to be Colson." He looked back to me.

"Yes sir, and congratulations. Welcome home Miss Whitmore. My name is Lily, just say my name if you need me."

"Thank you Lily." I remember Daisy well enough to not be surprised completely, but I am in awe. "Lou." I gave him that scolding look children are used to. "What other surprises are you full of?"

He pointed to the fried chicken. "I can cook."

"We bought this meal prepared by the grocery store."

"I heated it up." He argued taking a big bite.

"Oh! My rump!" I felt the floor heat flare up then die down a little.

"Sorry. I should warn you Lily is our prototype with a sense of humor. She's harmless, but she does tend to find little ways to amuse herself."

"I didn't think it was possible for computers to have a sense of humor."

"It's not, if anyone asks. When you marry me I'll tell you all my little secrets. Until then, just don't mention Lily, or Daisy, to anyone. Okay?"

"I doubt anyone would believe me if I did." I laughed. "She's not going to watch us . . . later . . . is she?"

"No honey. She maintains video surveillance outside, but inside she's on a sleep mode unless her name is mentioned."

"Good. It's still a little weird."

"You'll get used to it. We'll use blankets until you do." He hinted and winked over another big bite.

"Don't put so much in your mouth. Pig." I teased taking a lady-like size bite from the back piece. The back is the tastiest piece of a fried chicken. There's not much meat, but the flavor makes up for it.

He made snorting noises and leaned into me with his cheeks full as he chewed.

"Oh!! You're such a . . . man. Quit!" I laughed and pushed him back.

He swallowed easier than I thought possible and chased it with a beer and a smile. "My polite little belle. That's what I should call you. Belle."

"Don't even think about it. If you need to give me a nickname, use the one I'm used to."

"Which is?" He's intrigued now.

"Bobby."

"Bobby?? That's a guys name. Forget it. I'll stick to Barbara."

"Fine by me."

"Who started that nickname?"

"I'm not sure. I think it was one of the girls in grade school. It stuck with me until the academy."

"Do you miss this academy?"

"Every day." I admitted. "Until recently. It was home. School was always home. Now you are."

He fed me a bite of macaroni salad. "I will always be your home. Speaking of which. I hope you have an eye for decorating."

I finished my bite before replying, "We'll do it together so you get what you like. I have a friend from school that might be able to help. I've always thought Cassandra had a good eye for decor."

"Works for me. We have tomorrow off. Want to go sailing?"

"Sailing?? Are you serious??"

"Sure. I have a buddy who owns a charting business. He'll hook us up."

"Can you sail?" This man is just full of surprises!!

"Yes, I have my captain's license. I work for him from time to time. The money is okay, but I go more for the sail."

"Captain Lou Colson. That has a beautiful ring to it."

"Thank you. I prefer Mrs. Barbara Rose Colson myself, but that's just me."

"Ha ha. I would love to go sailing with you tomorrow. You surprise me too Mr. Colson. Captain Colson."

"Ooh, I could get used to you calling me that." He smiled before biting back into his chicken.

We have to drive a ways to the far side of Seattle to get to the harbor. This time the ride is a lot easier because we're in a comfortable SUV. Lou said it was so we could pack the cooler, but I'm sure he could have gotten the cooler onto his bike. Heck, he had our whole lives on there yesterday.

"Thank you for driving today instead of riding. I want to ride again, but the break is much needed."

"You're allowed. Even seasoned riders get sore. They make a butt paste for that, but I think epsom salts works best. We'll pick you up some on the way home. With the truck we can do some real shopping."

"You need furniture as much as you need food."

"We baby. We." He corrected.

"That's taking some getting used to. Sorry."

"That's alright. You teach me some manners and I'll teach you to trust me."

"Where is Myles by the way?"

"We'll see him tomorrow. The guys roped him into helping a member move."

"And he didn't balk??"

"Nah. I think Myles has found a new family baby." He glanced at me then kissed my hand. "Sorry."

"No, I want him to move on, to be happy. Poor guy. He's probably been horribly lonely for twenty-five years."

"Not anymore, besides, he had you. I'm sure that was good for him. If he really got his girlfriend killed like he said, it probably fucked him up pretty good."

"Language Lou." I scolded him out of habit. "Sorry. I suppose I shouldn't be a nagging fiance."

He laughed. "Nag all you want babe. Just as long as you're with me to nag at me."

"Are you going to stop transporting?" Speaking of nagging. "It's dangerous, and probably the one thing I'll nag you to quit."

"Don't worry about it. I have some regulars I'll have to deal with, so be patient, but I'll wind that down and pick up more architectural jobs. I have people waiting three years in line already, so don't worry about money."

"I'm not worried about money silly. I'm worried you'll be bored sitting at home all the time with a desk job. Why else would you do it?"

"Ah. I should explain. Transporting paid for college. It was tricky, and took me almost twice as long, but I did it. All those years of transporting made me good at it. The club is where I get my work, so they take a cut. They need the money more than I do these days, so I kept at it. They'll understand me retiring. It happens."

"My husband the architect biker. Sounds so sexy." I think I'm in a dream.

"What exactly did you study in school?"

"Business. I have multiple boring degrees. If you ever want to start your own architectural firm, I'm your woman." I joked.

He kept looking at me, then the road.

By the fourth time I asked, "What?"

"Want to?"

"Start an architectural firm together??" I think my eyebrows have helium in them they rose so high. "Are you serious?"

"Why not? I know I'm good. I'd bet the house you're better. You do the money and scheduling, I'll take care of the rest?"

"Ah . . . wow. Yes, of course I'd love to do that with you. Is it wise to mix our personal relationship with business?"

He smiled that wicked boyish smile, "I like bickering with you Miss Whitmore. I look forward to you challenging me."

"You challenge me right back Mr. Colson. In so many ways." I looked out the window and let my mind wander a bit. So much has changed so fast. Is this my new home? This city? I like this city. It's busy, colorful, and seems old without feeling antique. It reminds me of an old picture Michelle showed me once of her and her parents under a Christmas tree.

It occurred to me then that I don't have any pictures of myself with my father. Mr. Whitmore. Why did he raise me. He didn't raise me. He paid other people to do so. Why?

"Barbara? What's wrong honey?"

I wiped a tear away, "Why did Mr. Whitmore bother with me? Why not just ship me off to the system? Why did he put me through fancy schools and all but give me his family home if he wasn't my father?"

"Let's find out." He hit a button on the mirror. "Lily, get me Myles Carlson. The number is in my phone."

Two minutes later Myles' familiar voice is in the air. "Hey kid. How's Lou treating you?"

"Wonderfully. We're getting married."

"Good, I won't have to kick his ass. Listen, I've been in touch with the lawyers. We've got some paperwork to deal with, but not until Monday. Are you coming with Lou to the Poker Run this weekend?"

"I, uh." I laughed, "I don't know."

"Yeah, we'll be there. Barbara wants to ask you something about Mr. Whitmore, Myles."

"Oh, alright. What do you want to know?"

"Why did he keep me?"

"Keep you?"

"Yeah. Why did he pay for my schooling and pamper me with all those luxuries if he resented I wasn't his?"

"He never resented you Barb. You look exactly like your mother, the woman he loved with all his heart. When your mother was killed he sank into a dark hole. I don't think he ever made it out."

"She was killed?"

"Shit. I thought you knew that."

"They told me it was complications from giving birth to me."

"I'm sorry kid, those complications were Paulie. He didn't want her to take him for child support. With her dead, nobody would even think about him as your father. Mr. Whitmore knew, but he kept it to himself. That is until recently. I think he tried to blackmail Paulie to expose you. He was being cornered about losing the eight million dollar deal. I guess he thought he could use that to protect himself from Paulie. The details are a little sketchy, but that's the gist."

"Do we still have his ashes?"

"Yes. I have them with me. Well, at the hotel."

"Okay. Keep them. I have some thinking to do."

"Hey Barb?"

"Yeah?" I sniffled.

"People make mistakes. We don't always know the reasons, and sometimes there just aren't any. Remember how you used to preach forgiveness a couple years ago?"

I laughed through my tears as Lou pulled over into a residential area. "Yeah. I remember. My Bible thumping days."

"Forgive Barbara. It's not worth holding on to that level of bitterness. You have Lou, and once you get used to these crazy ass bikers, you'll have a real family. Trust me."

His words broke me into raking sobs.

Lou hopped out of the truck and came around to open my door and hug me tight.

"You got her Lou?"

"I do buddy. Thanks. She's okay. I'll call you back in a bit. I'm taking her sailing this afternoon if my phone goes out."

"Good, she'll like that." I heard the tone as Myles hung up first.

Lou rocked me in his embrace. "It's okay babe. I got ya. Shhhh. It's okay. I won't let anyone hurt you again."

I hugged him hard before peeling back and looking up, "I love you so much. I'm sorry to cry on you like this."

"Stop apologizing sweetheart. You're allowed to cry, you've been through a lot." He wiped a tear from my cheek with his thumb. "I love you Barbara. We'll get through this, then we'll build a life together where you don't have to look over your shoulder, and I get to sip sweet tea made by my sexy wife while I work to put our six kids through college."

I laughed hard enough to wash away the sadness that seemed to consume me so quickly. "Six kids??"

"Seven?"

"No way!! Do you know what children do to a woman's body??"

He smiled and put his hand on my belly, "Yeah, they make a pretty lady a beautiful woman. Our children will be well loved, by both their parents."

"You don't really want six kids, do you??"

"I want what you want." He kissed me sweetly then set me back in my seat. "Let's go sailing. I want to kiss you naked on the bow."

"What??" I heard my voice crack as he smiled and shut the door. When he got back in and us on the road I asked him. "You don't really expect me to get naked on your boat do you?"

"Maybe not, but we're definitely going to have some fun. We'll play it by ear." For the rest of the drive we talked about ideas for the architectural firm. He said he knows two other guys that would be willing to work with us too.

Evidently Lou is a very sought after architect. I Googled a couple buildings he designed on his phone and found myself impressed once more. This kept us talking until he parked at the harbor.

For the next twenty minutes I watched as he talked to people he seems to have known his whole life. He introduced me as his fiance to more people than I'll remember, but they all seemed very nice, and funny. Everyone joked and laughed freely as they worked to get the supplies on the boat. I offered to help but was told to stand back so I didn't fall in. Since I don't have much experience around boats or water I stepped back.

Lou helped me step on board and held up a life jacket, "Can you swim?"

"Yes."

"Good, put this on."

"Why did you ask me if I could swim if I have to wear this?" I took it anyway and pulled it around my shoulders.

"Makes me feel better taking you out on the water if I know you can swim."

"Would you have cancelled the trip if I said no?"

He swatted my hands away and tightened the straps. "No, but I would have stayed closer to shore. Now we can go out a little bit further. For privacy." He tightened the last strap and teased my lips with his before leaving me wanting and taking my hand to pull me down into the body of the boat.

"You give me butterflies when you talk like that."

He led me to a seat over his left shoulder at the wheel. "Good to know. Sit there until we get out of the harbor."

"Aye aye Captain." I sat down and pulled my feet under my tush. This is nice already and we haven't left the dock.

He started and engine as he smiled at me, "Keep talking dirty to me like that and we'll never get out of the slip."

"You look really happy Lou. Like you love this." It's written all over his face.

He looked past me and held the large wheel as he moved a lever with the other hand and backed us out of the space. Slip. I should brush up on my nautical terms. Obviously this is a passion for Lou. "I love you." He replied before turning around to take us slowly through the no wake zone. Hey, I remembered that one!

Since we were moving so slowly I stood up and wrapped my arms around his middle. Surely he can't get mad at me for this. I'm holding onto him like on the motorcycle, only this seems much safer.

He pulled me around and put my hands on the wheel. He pointed to a spot on the horizon. "See that buoy?"

"The orange one?"

"Yes. Drive towards it. I'll control the speed. Keep your hands on the wheel."

"Why am I getting butterflies again?" I asked nervously, but curious at the same time.

He moved my hair away from my neck as his hands moved to my hips. "Keep your eyes open." He unfastened my jeans without me feeling it. I felt his hand though. I panicked and looked around. Okay. Nobody can see.

"You're bad." I scolded him trying to match the point at the front of the boat with the target he'd given me.

"You're beautiful." He whispered in my ear. "Are you paying attention to where you're going?"

"Yes. So far."

"Good." He worked my jeans down to make room for his hand. It's almost too far, but we're still alone, so I let it go. "Don't let us crash Barbara. I'm trusting you." He became more intense with his movements in my jeans and I had to fight the urge to lean back and close my eyes to succumb to his expertise.

I gripped the wheel and focused on the buoy ahead as my body shattered once more at his touch and my knees went weak. Good thing I'm holding the wheel. "Wow."

He fixed my jeans as he kissed my neck. "You are one sensual woman Barbara. I was concerned I might wear you out on our honeymoon, but I'm beginning to think it's going to be you who wears me out."

I stepped aside to get a kiss. When I got my reward I smiled up at his beautiful profile. Strong jaw. Sailor's jaw? Maybe. Smooth sloped nose with a slight bump at the end you don't notice right away. He's wearing sunglasses, but I know those blue eyes are in there. Probably very proud of himself right about now. I've seen that look before.

I leaned into him as he pulled me under his arm and drove us slowly out of the no wake zone. I giggled when I realized we're like honeymooners. We haven't even put up the sails and we're making out. That was fun.

So was the rest of the day. He worked that boat like he works my body. With finesse and expertise. I stood, or sat, in awe of him most of the day. We enjoyed a picnic lunch as the boat drifted freely for a while. I got to take my life vest off for a while, but it cost me a good upper body massage.

I didn't mind once the initial shyness wore off. I've never been topless outside the bathroom, or bedroom. It seems I'm a little braver than I thought.

On the drive home I yawned, "That was wonderful Lou. Thank you for today. I know I owe you one, but I'm afraid you keep tapping my energy . . . by . . . nightfall." I looked at him, "Are you wearing me out on purpose??"

He moved his lower jaw back and forth a couple times, "Maybe a little."

"Why??"

"Oh boy."

"What?? Just tell me." I insisted.

"There's a couple reasons."

"I'm listening."

"One of them is very selfish. The other is for you."

"Lou." It was a warning to get on with his explanation.

"If you're exhausted you sleep better."

"And? The selfish reason is?"

He glanced at me, "If you're asleep I'm less inclined to start kissing you, which could easily lead up to a lot more. We need to get you on birth control."

"I agree, and I'm just teasing you here, but weren't you the one just talking about having six kids?"

"Not today, geeze. Give a guy a minute. You can't rush men into these things you know. We're a slow bunch." Now he's teasing me.

"Right, that's why after almost two weeks you're ready to marry me."

"Like I said, we're slow." He kissed my hand and winked at me.

12

Later that evening, I stood with my hands on my hips looking around the large empty space that is his house. "Where do we start?"

Lou is leaning against the kitchen bar freshly showered and drinking a beer straight from the bottle. "We? Don't get me involved." He teased. Although I get the feeling he'd let me do whatever I wanted with his house.

I held my hand out, "May I see your phone?"

"Calling Decor 911?" He picked the phone from his jacket pocket that's resting on the same counter he's leaning on and set it in my palm.

"No, I'm going to take a few pictures so when we go out tomorrow to buy, or order, furniture I'll have a reference."

"Smart." He agreed. "I need to check in at the club tomorrow, then we'll shop until you drop."

"Will Myles be there?"

"Yeah, he got there yesterday."

"What do you think he'll do about Paulie?"

"We're putting together a crew right now. That's what the meeting is about tomorrow. Just to prepare you, there will be two prospects following you around at all times. We can't be together twenty-four seven now that I'm home. For now Myles and I will try to take turns being your body guard, but because it's the mob we're putting backup in the wings. You don't want to underestimate the mob."

"Better safe than sorry. I would really like this to be over with so we can move on with our lives." I complained.

"I know honey. When we see Myles tomorrow you two can discuss the details of how to handle the companies."

"I want to sell off everything as soon as possible. Before the feds start digging too deep. That way I can hand over whatever files they want and wash my hands of the whole ordeal."

"And if you're too late?"

I shrugged, "Then I'll deal with it. I'm just thinking if I don't have an active role in the shady businesses then they can't accuse me of the same crimes as my father. It will be easier to believe I had nothing to do with this mess if this goes to court. I don't think I'd fit in very well at some women's correctional facility." I shuttered at the idea.

"I'd never let that happen. You're a smart lady my love. What about the house?"

"I'm going to make sure it's financially stable, then split it up for the employees. Give them each equal shares until my name is no longer on it. Let them buy each other out until it's down to who really wants to keep it. It was never much of a home, just a home base." I waved for him to follow me to his bedroom.

"Did you get that in Vegas?" After showering, I had put on some of my new clothes that he helped pick out.

"Yes. You like?" I smiled knowing he's watching my rear end.

"How tired are you?", he said with that wicked grin of his.

The shower had given me a second wind. "Let me finish these pictures and you can Ahh!!! LOU!!!" I screamed because he surprised me buy scooping me up into his arms. I almost dropped his phone. "What are you doing??"

"You can take pictures in the morning. Right now I want to feel your naked skin against mine while I kiss you all over."

I put my arms around his neck as he set me on my feet beside the sleeping bag that's still on the floor of the living room. "I love you."

"I love you sweetheart." He cupped my face for a second, then drove his long fingers into my hair as he tilted my head back lifting my chin. Bright blue eyes looked deeply into mine and I'm sure he can see straight into my soul. "I think we should get married on a sailboat."

"You do?" That was unexpected.

"The way you looked on that boat today, with the wind in your hair, and your eyes closed to the peaceful caress of the sun. I will forever have that image of you in my head. An image to conjure on a bad day when I need a smile."

"You could just come find me for a kiss on bad days." I leaned into him and locked my arms around his middle. He's lean, but strong. I can feel his muscles move slightly under my arms.

"I'm going to be finding you for kisses everyday for the rest of my life." He closed in and kissed me until clothes seemed to remove themselves as the passion ignited between us. Damn birth control. I'd welcome him tonight. I think I know where we need to go first tomorrow.

"A free clinic?? No baby, I'll call Doc. He writes all the girls scripts."

"I'm not sure I like the sound of that." I broke off a piece of banana nut muffin and popped it into my mouth. Lou and I decided we should get out of the solitude of his house. Too much time alone was going to tempt us a little too much. I'm not ready for children. Yet.

"It's no big deal. I don't want you going to some nasty clinic. Doc has a real office and everything. He just happens to be a member too."

"I don't like the idea of one of your friends seeing my goodies."

Lou spit coffee all over the table.

I grabbed napkins and started wiping, "Are you okay? Did you choke?"

He's laughing harder than I could have imagined. It's a fascinatingly display of male happiness I'll spend the rest of my life trying to elicit from him as often as possible. Although for the life of me I can't figure out what he's laughing so hard about.

"Lou?"

He finally settled down and sat back with his hand over his stomach as he caught his breath. "Did you just refer to your girly parts as 'goodies'?"

"Oh, I wondered what was wrong with you. Yes, I did. I don't care for the more vulgar terms."

"Such as?" He's messing with me hoping I'll say one those foul words.

"No way. I am a lady, and ladies do not talk that way. I would rather you didn't use those vulgar terms when talking to me about my goodies either."

He chuckled again. "You are so damn cute. Okay, no vulgar sex talk." He leaned forward and picked up my hand to play in his. "You're going to keep me on my toes, aren't you?"

I smiled and squeezed his hand, "If you let me, yes."

"I look forward to it." He leaned in closer and kissed my hand. "Finish your breakfast. We need to get to the club soon."

"Yes dear." I replied sarcastically to scold him for his bossiness.

"Please." He added giving me a look that told me he was teasing me.

"This is your 'club'??"

"Well, it is now. Our old club got bull-dozed because of residential expansion a few years ago."

"They just bull-dozed it??"

"Might as well have. The state offered up fair market value, which was shit because of the economy. Cracker Jacks is still pissed, so don't bring it up."

"Cracker Jacks?"

"The President of this chapter. He's the General's son. General retired about five years ago. You'll meet him today I'm sure, this is his and his wife's place. You'll like Liz."

"This place is a mansion, almost like yours but yours is more modern, and has a lot more windows, but just as big."

"Jacks invested in Microsoft before anyone knew who they were." He didn't knock, just opened the large ornate front door. "This is home away from home for me. Relax Barbie, some rich people are cool." He's enjoying my surprise and confusion.

"Please don't call me Barbie in here." I begged stepping just inside the large foyer.

"What would you prefer to be called? Barbara seems little stuffy for the biker world."

"Bobby."

"Bobby?" He put his hand on my lower back as I looked up and around.

"Yes. It's a fairly common nickname for Barbara, and easier to cheer for than Barbara."

"Cheer for?"

"Myles would cheer for me when I tried my hand at sports. Evidently I'm much better with a gun than a ball."

He wrapped his arms around my middle and kissed my neck from behind me. "I beg to differ. Or should I say, my balls beg to differ."

I elbowed him playfully, "Lou!!"

He laughed and turned me in his arms. "Hey, I didn't say one vulgar word."

I laughed and felt a little bit more relaxed being in this large stranger's house. "You're pushing it."

"Yes, and you love it. Come on, let's go downstairs. This house sits on a steep hill. The basement is actually where you get out to the backyard. That's where the club moved to until we couldn't find another spot."

"His wife let him put this sign up?"

He opened a normal looking interior door with a sign on the front that read, 'Warning. Keep out unless you have really big boobs.' "It keeps drunk bikers from opening wrong doors all over her house."

I giggled. "I think I like her already."

We descended two levels of stairs that rounded a corner. I looked around taking in the scene. "It looks like a sports bar."

"A lot of times it is. The guys like to bet and grill. You'll find we have a lot of excuses to throw parties." He ushered me slowly over to a large table of eight that sat six at the moment.

A large portly man with salt and pepper red hair and bright green eyes stood and took Lou's hand. "Welcome back Bro." He took my hand next, "You must be Barbie. I'm Jacks."

"Bobby, and yes. Nice to meet you Jacks." His grip was firm, but not too hard. He was a gentleman, but didn't treat me like I was to gentle for a real shake.

I was introduced to the rest of the table before Lou walked me over to the bar and sat me in the corner at the end. "Sorry to abandon you in a strange place baby. I'll be as quick as I can, but you can't be in on this meeting. If you need me just wave your hand in the air. I'll just be right over there."

"I'm a big girl Lou. Go have your meeting."

He cupped my face and kissed me possessively. Good. That should keep men from hitting on me. Although I'm sure I'm not their type. Come to think of it, they wouldn't know that from the way I'm dressed. Oh well. When he pulled back he said, "I have an open tab here, get whatever you want. Blue usually keeps newspapers behind the bar if you want to catch up on current events."

"That's not a bad idea. Take your time Lou. I wouldn't mind a little while to soak all this in."

"Thank you love." He stole one more kiss then left me for his meeting across the room.

The bartender, who introduced himself as Blue, stepped up wiping his hands on a dishtowel. "Can I get you something to drink?"

"Yes please, do you have iced tea?"

"I do."

"I heard a rumor you might have a current newspaper hidden behind this beautiful bar." I hinted.

"I have several." He hooked me up with fresh iced tea, sugar, and three different newspapers. I read, sipped, and people watched for probably an hour. The time didn't drag as there was a lot to take in.

A few of the women gave me that typical territorial look women give when they feel their turf is being tread upon. Knowing I'm the new girl on the block I just gave a polite smile and went back to reading. Maybe once they realize the only man I'm after is Lou, and not theirs, they'll warm up.

Myles walked in from outside and I all but fell off my stool to crash into him, "MYLES!!!" Okay, that was completely undignified, but I can't help it.

He hugged me hard and spun me around twice. "Hey kid. Miss me?"

He set me on my feet and I stepped back, "You have no idea how much I missed you."

"Lou been treating you right?" He looked around for Lou.

"Oh yes! It's not that. I just missed you. Wow." I stepped back. Myles is wearing chaps and a black leather vest. Gone is the suit and tie. "You look, amazing."

He turned around and showed me the back of his jacket. "Looks like I found a new cause." It read *Prospect* across the bottom.

"I'll say you did. Are you happy??"

He took my arm and we went to the bar to catch up and talk about what to do with my father's, I mean, Mr. Whitmore's, assets. Maybe I should go back to referring to him as my father. He's not so bad when compared to Paulie.

We decided to put everything up for sale after a quick fix of the books. Pay off any debts, no matter who the loanee, and make sure any illegal operations are ceased immediately. Then put them on craigslist.com and have us a fire sale.

As far as Paulie was concerned we decided to let the club check things out first. Slider said he would look into what happened and pull some strings for information. Two weeks should be enough time for him to settle this matter peacefully.

"If he can't, tell him I'll pay the eight million. I have that in cash."

"It doesn't work that way. Paulie is going to assume you'll keep paying money to avoid starting a war. You're a woman. Soft hearted."

"What do we do?"

"I'm not sure. Aside from bankrupting your cash supply so there's nothing to come after, I don't know."

"So I can't give the money to him, and I can't keep it?"

"Right, at least he can't think you have it"

"I need a drink." Blue set a shot glass on the bar in front of me. "Whiskey, please."

"You still run the risk of pissing him off if you give the money away. Best to let him think the Feds got it all if we can."

"True." I downed the shot and chased it with my tea. "Bleck."

Myles laughed. "You look good kid. Biker clothing suits you better than those ugly grey suits."

"Yeah, I can't say as I miss the stockings either." I scratched my leg.

"How's things with you and the other biker in your life?"

"Good. We're getting married, someday. There's no date set, just rings We put them away for a fancier proposal, but had a private one between us. He's rather sweet under that scruffy young beard." I laughed and waved off the offer of a second shot.

"He'll be good for you. But if he ever gets out of line you call me, I'll come kick his ass back in shape." He promised.

"Deal. Are you going to show me your bike?"

"Absolutely." We went upstairs and out front where all the bikes were neatly parked in short rows of five or six in the front yard. That poor grass.

A little while later Myles had to go run an errand with another prospect so I went back to the bar. A woman with medium length light brown hair in a ponytail turned on her barstool as I walked over. "Barbara?"

"That's me." I replied cheerfully. She has happy puppy dog brown eyes. I doubt this woman could make an enemy if she tried.

She held her hand out, "I'm Liz, Cracker Jacks wife."

I shook her hand eagerly, "Oh! It's so nice to meet you!"

She beckoned Blue over as I sat down beside her at the bar. After ordering a cup of coffee she turned back to me. "How are you adjusting?"

"So far so good. I'm definitely out of my element, but I seem to be meeting the most friendly people."

She smiled proudly, "Yes, we are more like a big family. We have our squabbles and issues, but the love is always there for each other. Would you like to go up and check out my big fancy house while these guys finish their business?"

"I would love to. From what I've seen it's lovely. Even your biker bar basement is lovely. I could have never pulled this off." I stood with her as we gathered our drinks and headed for the stairs.

"Sounds like you'll be doing some decorating soon." She hinted for more information. That's all it took. Liz became my best friend over the next hour.

We ended up having a lot in common. Her family is from Virginia, so she understands a little about southern culture. We also have similar taste in decor, so she gave me phone numbers and names of places to shop. On our way back down to the guys we exchanged phone numbers and promised to go shopping on Monday.

I promised to talk to Lou and make sure it was okay for me to come by tomorrow morning and let me help her and the other girls set up for the big party after the Poker Run Saturday morning. She explained that most people wouldn't get here until around dinner time, but the pre-party was nothing to dismiss either. Those who can't ride in the run for whatever reason come help out and get the festivities started.

Lou was standing in a small group of bikers when I saw him. His smile went ear to ear and tugged at my heart strings. He met me halfway and quickly put his arm around my back and pulled me against him for a long possessive kiss.

I let him get away with it for a few seconds before I remembered where we are. "Lou, behave. People are watching."

"Oooh, kinky." He teased and nipped my neck playfully. While he was by my ear he asked, "Ready to go shopping?"

"Yes, please."

He stood upright and set concerned light blue eyes on mine, "Did you enjoy your visit with Liz?"

"Oh yes, for sure. We've exchanged numbers so we can get together on Monday. I just missed you, that's all."

"So you're okay here? Not scared?"

"No, not scared at all. It's kind of like the first day of school, but it takes a lot more than that to put me out. Would you rather stay here than shop with me?" It just dawned on me shopping may not be up this biker's alley.

"I'd rather be with you wherever you are. Besides, I need to make sure you don't put up pink lace and buy ugly fuzzy pillows." He teased and waved to the guys.

I waved too before he escorted me up the stairs. "Do I look like the fuzzy pillow type to you?"

He filled his hands with my tush and squeezed. "I like these pillows."

I swatted his hands away. "Remind me not to walk up stairs in front of you."

"Remind me to melt butter on those sweet biscuits later."

"Lou!!" I had to laugh though. He's having too much fun working around the definition of vulgarity with his talk of biscuits. I like the way he thinks. He's risky fun with his words. My beautiful, tall, sliver-tongued biker is going to be keeping me on my toes as well.

"Don't you think that's a little big Lou?" He'd just flopped down on the biggest, fanciest, mahogany four-post bed I've ever seen. The ornate twisted posts really would go nicely against the sharp angles of his large windows.

"I'm a big guy." He argued.

I studied the linens. "It is beautiful, and yes, you are a big guy. It just seems a little, excessive."

"You don't like it?" He rolled to his side and propped up on his elbow to reach for me, "Come here."

"No way." I jumped back. "You're dangerous in beds."

"Dangerous?" He's loving this.

"Yes, and floors." I wiggled his booted foot as I walked around to look at the rest of the bedroom set.

"You should lay down on a mattress before you buy it."

"I'll trust your judgement." I opened drawers. The light marble tops are beautiful. I'm in love with this set. It's intimidating in it's beauty. Kind of like Lou. His eyes are intimidatingly cold one minute, and sparkling happily the next.

"Wow. You trust me??" He rolled over and tried to catch my arm again. "Barbara, get over here. You know I'll come get you." He threatened.

I turned back around to face him, "You better not!!"

He started to get off the bed.

I ran over and sat on the edge. "Okay! Behave. I'm here."

He lunged and next thing I know I'm being tickled on top of this huge bed in the middle of this very nice furniture store.

"Lou!! Stop!!" I grabbed his ears finally.

He laughed and hopped off the bed to help me up. He looked at the sales lady who appeared suddenly. "We had to give it the tickle test. Very important." He assured her making me giggle.

I hid behind Lou as she replied sternly, "I suppose that we're lucky that's the only test you two have in mind. Are you interested in this bed?" A huge smile on her face gave her away.

"I want the whole set. When can you deliver?"

"We can order the set today and have it to you in about two weeks."

"Fine." He looked over his shoulder at me, "Okay?"

I nodded still completely embarrassed.

He looked back to her, "What do you have in living room furniture?"

13

"You want to leave at what time in the morning??" Lou asked as we carried bag after box after bag after box into the house. We'd come back here to get his truck after ordering the furniture.

"I want to help. There is a ton of cooking to do and coolers to fill. I had no idea what kind of work goes into these biker parties of yours." I teased using my foot to hold the door open for him.

"Thanks. I know it's a lot of work to put on a multi-chapter rally, but I wanted to sleep in tomorrow."

"You have no intention of sleeping Mr. Colson, but nice try. Don't you have work to do tomorrow or something?" Tomorrow is Friday. I'm losing track of days here.

"I do have a draft I need to get done, but that's not the point. We'll be apart." He complained looking around. "This room just got a lot smaller."

I took his hand to drag him to the garage for another load, "Oh hush. Once it's unpacked and put away it will be a nice open space again. Do you mind if I drive your truck tomorrow?"

"No. Yes. No. Of course not, take the truck." He's pouting and all but stomping his feet in protest to my plans.

It made me smile. "You can come with me." I offered.

"Right. That's what I want to do. No thanks. I'll catch up on some work. It'll make my client happy." He conceded.

We finished unloading the truck then stopped to drink beers before attempting to unpack. I cleared a spot and sat on the counter because my feet can't take anymore.

"Tired baby?" He sauntered over to stand between my knees.

"Yes, thank you very much. Do you really have to have top of the line everything? Or were you wearing me out again?"

"A little of both. I like quality." He seemed perfectly at home as he took a long draw from his beer.

"Why are you still trying to wear me out? Myles and I talked, we have a sensible plan. If all goes well with the help of your club we should be able to settle this peacefully."

"Birth control. I made an appointment for you tomorrow at eleven. You can follow me in the truck in the morning. You can text me if you need directions to Liz's, from the Doc's office."

"I don't have a phone."

"Liz didn't give you your stuff today?"

"She did, but there was no phone. I thought Myles told them to get rid of it for security reasons or something. I saw him before Liz, so I didn't know to ask."

"Ah. Okay. I have a couple pre-pays you can pick from. I'll get them from the safe while you unpack all this crap."

"You spent a fortune today." I scolded him because he really did insist on buying the best of the best. It was hard to keep up with at times, and frustrating when he couldn't find the 'exact' thing he was looking for. I finally put myself in the frame of mind to just sit back and enjoy the ride. Note to self, never take Lou shopping again. I wonder now if he did this on purpose. Something to file away for another day.

He shrugged. "I can afford it. Speaking of which, I need your wallet."

"You're robbing me??" I teased reaching over and sliding my purse closer. I have no secrets, and when he runs across the tampon I might get a good laugh.

"Yes, as a matter of fact, I am. Don't touch your money yet. Not personally. If anyone asks it's just a precaution in case your father's shit rolls downhill. You don't want to be accused of spending money obtained illegally. It will also help in court." He gave me a knowing look before continuing to empty my wallet.

"Sounds good to me, but we think about that business we talked about soon so I pay you back. I will not be a kept woman."

He narrowed his eyes and pulled out a picture I'd almost forgotten was in there. "What's this??"

I snatched it from his fingers and shoved it in my bra. "That's my fantasy husband, or was, now I have a new one, and he's a lot cuter."

He dove in after the picture overpowering me easily. He flicked the picture of Johnny Depp dressed as Captain Jack Sparrow over his shoulder. "No more pictures of other men in your wallet." He's doing a pretty good job of looking jealous.

"I'll have to replace it with one of you."

"Just make sure I don't look like a fucking pirate."

"Ooh, kinky." I echoed his words and got swept into a long sweet kiss. His phone rang before we sunk to the floor for some serious heavy petting.

While he talked in the other room I began unpacking. It's like Christmas in this kitchen right now. I love it!! Okay, knives first, or the scissors, whichever comes first.

We ordered pizza because after unpacking and taking the trash out we were exhausted. I fell asleep with my head on Lou's lap, but woke up in his arms.

I looked up from under his arm, "I have to pee, and your leg is locked around me."

He tightened his grips and hugged me close. "I don't wanna go to school Ma."

I laughed and tried to tickle his ribs. "I'll tinkle on you."

He caught my hands and slowly set them above my head capturing my wrists in one hand and placing his other hand flat on my stomach. His eyes are playful blue with a sprinkle of mischief. "Want to know a secret?"

"Probably not, but now I must know. Do tell."

"It's better when your bladder is full." He hinted.

"What is . . . oh . . . it gets better??"

He smiled, "Want to find out?"

"I'm nervous." I confessed.

"Don't be nervous. Just don't tinkle."

I squealed in laughter as he tightened his grip on my ankles, I had both legs now bent up at the knees, and hooked his leg over my right leg after he unfolded it.

He waited until I caught my breath, "Open for me." He instructed as his fingers walked down my thigh.

I let my left knee fall away and tried to pull my hands free from his grip over my head. "Lou, let go."

He touched his nose to mine, "No. If you're going to leave me all day I want to play. Just relax, I'm only going to touch and kiss you. Let go and enjoy Miss Whitmore." He urged as he found me all too moist and ready for his affection.

He must have changed my clothes after I'd fallen asleep because I suddenly realized I'm wearing one of his t-shirts and just my panties. As he caresses me towards release I can feel him pulling my shirt up with his teeth.

As soon as he found and sucked my nipple into his mouth my body exploded in his hand. "Oh Lou!!!"

"Wait, you're not done." He pushed those two magic fingers into me and did something deep inside me that brought me right back up, and uncontrollably over into another glorious wave of ecstasy. Why do couples get out of bed again?? Oh yeah, food.

My stomach growled making us both laugh. It didn't take long to return the favor for my fiance, so I managed to make it to Doc's only ten minutes late, then headed directly to Liz's.

The kitchen was an assembly line of tasks. Cut this, dice that, slide these, and stir that. I fell right into wherever they made room. Liz introduced me as she shouted orders to the other girls in the kitchen. Within an hour I was so engrossed in the cooking and the gossip my troubles seemed a lightyear away.

I've never laughed so hard in my life! The vulgar things voiced out of these ladies' mouths made Lou look like a choir boy. After the first fifteen blushes I finally relaxed and began laughing with them. Several times I told a shorter version of the story of how Lou and I met.

One girl, Evette, came over and stood a little too close. "Lou's been my regular for going on seven years. Not only are you costing me money, but if you don't treat him right I'll kick you ass. He's a good man."

I looked up into dark brown eyes, "I am well aware Lou is a good man. I apologize for your decline in finances, but as with any business, it comes, and it goes. And if you think you can kick my ass, I welcome the challenge. It's been a long time since I've had a good spar."

She bit the inside of her cheek and nodded, "I like you Barbie. Welcome to the family." She winked and left fanning her face. "Watch that one, she spits fire in the form of words." That got a good chuckle out of everyone before we moved on to another topic of conversation. Liz gave me an approving nod and smile. I suppose that means I've passed the test so to speak. I exhaled for the first time that day.

Lou snuck up on me just as the sun was about to set. We'd all decided it was margarita time on the back patio. I looked up over my right shoulder as his arms came around my middle. "Hey you. How was your day?"

"Boring. Yours?" He kissed my lips, then my jaw and now under my ear. I heard and felt him inhale slowly giving me shivers. "Oh wow. You smell like apple pie and Barbara. Let's go home now so I can have me some dessert."

I giggled and turned in his arms. "I missed you."

He stepped back looking me over and tucked my hair behind my ear. "You did huh?" He asked teasing me with those light sky blue eyes.

"You know I did Mr. Colson." I put my arms around his neck and pulled him down for a long sweet kiss. After all the things said in that kitchen today, I don't think kissing my man in front of the girls is going to be a big shocker. When we finally let go of each other I noticed a few other girls were welcoming their men in a similar fashion.

Every time I get on his motorcycle it feels more and more comfortable. He said not to worry about his truck, he'll send someone for it later. Riding as the sky darkens didn't frighten me anymore. I'm not sure I'm ready for long rides at night, but this twilight ride is nice. Romantic. I'm really happy Doc gave me that birth control shot earlier, it should be effective in less than two weeks.

I looked around inside his house and cringed. "I guess I didn't unpack as much as I thought."

"Don't worry about it. You have plenty of time to unpack. The rest of the furniture won't be here for a couple weeks, so we'll just have to pretend we're camping." He hung his jacket on of two barstools we'd bought just to get us through until the good ones arrive. He assures me he'll use them in the garage, so they won't go to waste.

He took my hand, "Come with me, I want to show you something."

"What did you do?" I asked like I was speaking to a troublesome child.

"You'll see." He stole a kiss from my lips before smiling and pushing open his bedroom door. "It's not fancy, but I thought you'd prefer an air mattress over a sleeping bag."

I stepped inside to find he'd made up the air mattress with white sheets and a dark blue comforter. On either side of the air mattress at the top where the pillows are piled are breakfast in bed trays, and mini nightstands for our things.

I looked up and hopped on my toes to put my arms around his neck, "Thank you, it's beautiful."

"I wouldn't say beautiful. You're beautiful." He argued and kissed me until we tripped, accidentally on purpose, onto the air mattress.

After a while I noticed he didn't seem to have the wondering hands I'm finding myself expecting. Okay, craving. I'm turning into a wanton woman in this man's care. I tried to encourage him by guiding his hands under my shirt.

He shook his head and lifted up, "No."

"No? Is something wrong?"

He raked his hand through his hair. "Yes, and no. Not with you, ever, at all. I'm trying to, figure something out."

"Talk to me."

He sighed and settled on his elbow beside me. "I think I want to wait."

"You think you want to wait, for what?" I touched his beard to gauge the days growth. It seems to be getting softer each time I touch it.

"To make love to you. Since this got serious I've been wondering what it would be like. To have that level of anticipation." He turned to look down at me and touched my cheek. "It never occurred to me that I'd have a virgin wife. The idea is more intriguing every day."

"You want to wait until we're married??"

He nodded, "I think I do. Unless you talk me out of it of course, but yes. I'd like to have that with you. We already know it's going to be fantastic. Tell me what you think. Am I crazy?"

I laughed, "Yes, but I love your kind of crazy. Are you sure about this??"

"We might have to get married two weeks and one day from now, but yes. I'm sure."

"After the day I had with your family today, I'd marry you right now."

He sat back in surprise, "Oh yeah?? Does that mean you had a good day?" He looks beautifully pleased. Lou happy is one handsome man. The smile alone melts my heart, add those eyes and I'm a puddle of goo at his feet.

I nodded, "Oh yes. It was wonderful. I was nervous at first. Evette and I had a nice little chat."

He smacked his forehead and fell to his back, "Oh no. I'm sure a douche."

"Lou." I can't help but laugh. Evette doesn't make me jealous. In fact, I respected her for caring enough about a man she took money from for sex to confront me.

"Go ahead, hit me. Beat me up. I'm so sorry. I'd completely forgotten about her."

"It's okay Lou. We had our words and ended up liking each other. She likes you. Now that she likes me she's happy to see you happy. It's not a problem, but I thought you should know we've met."

He opened one eye, "You're not mad?"

"Do I look mad?"

"No, you look amused. Why aren't you mad?"

"Because you told me before you didn't have time to date. I've learned a lot this last couple weeks. Especially tonight. What you did is not unusual. Not only that but at least you were careful, and honest. The oldest profession for women is not something I've ever had a problem with. I never understood it, and on some levels I still don't, but it's not for me to judge. Paying for sex is not like killing for money. I think I'll get over it."

"So, you and Eve are friends now?"

"Not friends, but we won't be catty when we're in the same room."

He rolled so I'm under him again. "I love you."

"I love you."

"I still want to wait."

"Two weeks and one day?"

He smiled ear to ear, "Two weeks and one day."

"There is no way I can plan a wedding inside of two weeks." I put my hand to my chest and popped another antacid. I'm not sure if they help or not.

"Bobby, you have got to calm down. You're face is bright red."

I touched my face, "It is?"

"Yeah, I think you should come lay down on the couch." Liz took my hand and led me to the large sofa in her front room. "Are you okay?"

"I think it's just nerves. Myles and I have been working feverishly to disband the companies. Then there's the wedding plans. I'm still looking over my shoulder for Paulie everywhere I go. Financially I'm busted flat. To be honest Liz, I think I'm drowning." I confided. We've spent the last couple days together since Lou is in desperate need of catching up on some work of his own.

She checked my forehead and my pulse. "I'm calling the doctor. Either you're having a nervous breakdown, or a heart attack."

"I'll be okay."

"No, I don't think so. You're going from red to green. I'm calling Lou." I remember feeling too tired to argue before everything went black.

"Lou, you need to go home and get some sleep." I think that's Liz.

"No. I'll sleep when she wakes up." Lou's voice sounds beaten. Tired. No. Exhausted.

I tried to squeeze his hand. I know it's his because only Lou's hand feels this way. His hand is the only hand I know better than I know my own.

"Barbara?" His voice cracked. "Baby, open your eyes, please."

It took me a couple tries and a minute to focus.

"Oh sweetheart. You scared the shit out of me." He started kissing my hand.

My throat is dry.

"Hang on, just a couple sips." He held a straw to my lips.

Oh my God I'm tired. It's so hard to stay awake, but I need to know what happened. It's obvious I'm in the hospital. "What happened?" It came out in a whisper.

"Just a little problem with your heart. The doctors took care of it, so you're okay now." Lou is lying his ass off.

"Don't. Just tell me."

Liz put her hand on Lou's shoulder. "Lou is right, you're okay now, but you had a virus. You have a virus, but they got it under control."

"A virus?"

"Yeah. He said you must have gotten it traveling. I forget the name of it, but it's a lifer. You can live a long happy life with it, but you have to keep your stress level way down. The stress is what gave it power to take you down sweetie." She explained perfectly.

I tested my neck and touched my heart. "I'm so tired. How long have I been here?"

"Too long." He looked up making me look over, "Hey Doc, she just woke up."

"I know, some big marine looking biker is out there raising hell." He checked my chart then walked over to shine a vicious light in my eyes. "Good. How do you feel Miss Whitmore?"

"Like I was hit in the chest by a truck."

"The virus shut your heart down pretty good. You died twice on the way here. Your chest hurts from the electrical shocks and the compressions. I'm putting you on bed rest for four weeks. Then you come in and we go from there. You'll be on medication the rest of your life, but the good news is you'll live a long happy life." He assured me.

"I died twice??"

"Yes. Don't dwell on that part. Dwell on the fact that you're alive to tell people that story. The nurse is going to give you something for the pain, which will help you sleep. Sleep a lot, it'll help you heal faster."

"When can I go home?"

"When I say so." He winked at me, "A couple days. In rare cases we have to put in a heart monitor. I don't think that will necessary in your case because you're so young and healthy, but I want to make sure before we send you home."

I nodded, "Thank you."

"Get some rest Miss Whitmore. You'll be out of here in no time." He pulled Lou and Liz aside for a brief chat before they came back over.

Lou took my hand and sat again, "Only one of us can stay, so Liz is going to go home now. Can she bring you anything?"

"No. Lou is going home, and I'll stay. You know her things better than I do, and you need some sleep. Go." She pointed to the door.

He simply dug his keys from his front jeans pocket and tossed them to her. "You know better."

Liz shook her head, "Fresh clothes and the usual toiletries?"

"Yes, please. Take Lou with you. I'm just going to sleep anyway."

Lou scooted his chair closer and put his head down on my thigh with my hand sandwiched in his.

"Never mind." I mouthed a 'thank you' before I moved his hair off his face. "Sleep sweetheart."

He moaned and snored lightly within seconds.

The nurse came in to put the pain medicine in the I.V. "I see he finally passed out." She said softly.

"How long have I been here?"

"Let me see." She checked my chart. "That's about right." She looked up, "Four days, this is your fifth night."

My face hurt at the pain poor Lou had suffered with me out cold from some heart virus brought tears to my eyes. Tears that overflowed uncontrollably.

"Hey." She touched my arm, "It's okay now. You're okay. And he's sleeping, finally. Try to relax, you don't want to relapse with stress, okay?"

I nodded and took a couple deep breaths that hurt like hell, but the pain helped chase away the hurt. "Thank you. Poor Lou. Has he been here the whole time?"

"Yes, and now that the doctor is off the floor I'm going to let your brother in. He's been driving us nuts."

I almost laughed, but it hurt too bad. "Myles?"

"Yes. Promise to stay calm?"

I nodded, "Yes, please. I want to see him."

Myles came in a few minutes later. He was too afraid to hug me, but he took me in and made sure I was okay before kissing both my cheeks, my forehead, and making me promise to rest and get better. Lou didn't budge except to keep his grip on my hand. Even in his sleep he won't let go for anything.

Life in a hospital stinks at best. If I'm lucky enough to sleep, somebody comes in to wake me up for vitals or shots. If I'm awake, I'm bored out of my ever living mind. No amount of magazines will sustain me.

Then there's Lou. "Please go home and take a shower. I'll still be here when you get back."

"I'm fine. You should be getting out of here tonight. I want to make sure I'm here to get you home."

"They're still doing the paperwork, and I have one more check-up before that happens. Not to be rude Lou, but you smell like four day old socks."

He laughed for the first time in a week then leaned over to kiss me and rub his stink all over my face and neck via his lips and beard. "Do i smell baby?"

I pushed his chest, but I'm still too weak to move him. "You quit. Pew Lou! My goodness you need some soap and a good scrub."

"Tell me about it." The doctor's voice interrupted our play.

Lou stood up, "Tell me you're kicking us out." He begged.

"I am. We need to talk first." He sat on the edge of my bed with the clipboard in his lap. He glanced at Lou, "You too."

Lou pulled up his chair, "I thought you said she was okay now Doc?"

"She is, but to stay that way you're going to have to follow a certain regime. First and foremost, no stress. Not even good stress, like a wedding. Keep it small." He eyed Lou.

"Done. What else?" Lou asked back.

The doctor looked at me, "No kids. In fact I strongly suggest you get a clamp put on your tubes so there's no accidents. If you get pregnant, it will kill you. Your heart is strong enough to keep you alive, but not two of you." He paused.

I sucked in and bit my dry lower lip. "No kids."

"That's right. I brought you some information on that clamp. I want to see you again in three weeks. We'll make any adjustments to your medications then. If you have any problems in the meantime my number is on the bottom of the first page. The key is rest. Bed rest for the next three weeks. If I clear you to get up you go on half day bed rest for a week." He pointed at my nose, "If you want a normal life, you'll take it easy and do not, get knocked up. I didn't save your life to trade it for an infant's."

"Who would take care of Lou?" I asked before I realized it was out loud.

He smiled as Lou squeezed my hand, "Keep that train of thought and you'll be fine." He stood leaving the papers behind. "The nurse will be here in a few minutes to help you into the wheel chair. Evidently you have quite the entourage waiting for you downstairs."

"I do?"

"Yeah. I've seen my share of bikers in this hospital, but this is ridiculous." He complained leaving me and Lou looking at each other.

I asked him, "How many people are here?"

He shook his head, "I haven't been out of this room since they brought in here. I have no idea."

"That explains why you smell like old socks."

The nurse rolled a wheelchair in with a smile, "Ready to go home Miss Whitmore?"

I looked at Lou, "My home seems be by my side wherever I am these days."

"These days, and all your days to come my love." He promised.

They wheeled me down the hall, down an elevator, down two more halls and out the front doors of the hospital. My face did that weird crunching thing as I took in the flood of motorcycles and bikers. My hand trembled over my mouth as Lou squatted down in front of me.

"You okay?" He wiped away my tears with his thumbs.

"There's so many!!" I laughed through tears. "Are they really all here for me??"

He nodded and sniffed back his own tears. "Yes baby. You're family. We're all here for you. Even Some Exiles came up to see you."

I really started crying then, "Oh my God!"

He pulled me into his arms for a gentle hug. "Shhh. Don't get too worked up. They''d never forgive themselves if their presence sent you back inside."

I wrapped my arms around his neck as he gently pulled me out of the chair and set me in the back seat of an SUV. "Please tell them thank you for me."

"Don't need to baby. Don't need to."

Two weeks later I was ready to kill him, and everyone else within shouting distance. If I have to spend one minute in this bed it's going to be somebody's last minute alive.

Lou walked in with a tray of tea and smile on his face. "Hello beautiful. How are you feeling?"

"Like I want out of this bed. Enough already."

"You might have gotten the okay from the doctor, but I'm not convinced. Just a few more days babe."

I threw the covers off and onto the floor. "No. I won't spend one more minute alone in this bed."

He set the tray on the dresser and walked over to take my hand. "Where do you think you're going?"

"Shopping."

"Shopping?? What for? Lay back down, I'll get it for you." He's driving me crazy with all this pampering.

"No!!" I pushed him away and stopped in the doorway, "Either get in that bed with me right now, or I'm going out to buy shoes."

"It's too soon. We've been over this. What if you have a heart attack during your first time? I don't think I could live with myself."

"I'm tired of waiting. I'm tired of waking up in the middle of the night alone because you've snuck out again. Stop trying to protect me and make love to me!!!"

"Okay, calm down. You're getting too worked up."

"I want to be worked up." I changed tactics. Something has got to work. I'll seduce this man if it's the last think I do, which at this rate could be a very long time. I stepped towards him and took my shirt off. "I'm done waiting."

"Barbara, don't."

"Go as slow as you want, but if you don't start undressing you I'll do it myself." I kicked out of my sweats and walked over backing him to the dresser. "I'm not that fragile. The dotter said I was cleared to have sex. You heard him yourself."

He put his hands on my hips. "We go slow, and you tell me the minute you feel sick or any pain. Promise?"

"Promise." I untucked his shirt and pulled it up over his head.

"Are you sure the IUD is working?"

"Yes."

"I don't want to get you

I put my finger to his lips, "Stop talking, and start kissing."

He narrowed those big blue eyes at me and smiled, "You're in trouble now Barbie."

"I've been in trouble since the day we met."

He backed me to the bed and climbed over me as I laid back with my head on the pillows. "I was dead before the day we met. I love you, with all my heart."

I reached down and took two handfuls of the muscular jean-clad tush I'm going to spend the rest of my life grabbing every chance I get. "I love you too." I pushed him to his back and popped the button of jeans open.

"Slow down."

"We've been going slow enough already. I've been stuck in this room with nothing but lusty thoughts of you for two weeks. No more daydreaming." I surprised myself as I took his jeans and boxers off and threw them to the floor.

He rolled to help me out of them bra and panties while spreading sweet warm kisses in his wake. His tongue flicked over the sensitive nub between my legs and I thought I'd rupture right then. "Not yet baby. Wait for me. I want to come with you."

He slid up and kissed me sweetly as his fingers found me more than ready. I reached down and began guiding him to my threshold.

He lowered onto his elbows and let me relax for a few seconds before lifting up breaking our kiss. His eyes are full of concern and desire. I can see the war raging inside him.

To ease the battle I smiled, "I'm okay Lou, more than okay."

He exhaled, "It's going to hurt for a minute, from what I understand."

"I'm well aware of that Lou. Come here." I drove my fingers through his hair and pulled him down so I can whisper in his ear. "I want you. Now. Please."

He pushed in just a little. "You're so tight." He's breathless with barely contained control.

I reached down, grabbed that perfect tush and dug my fingers in as hard as I could as I arched for him.

He groaned as he sunk deep and stopped. "Shit Barbie. If you move I'm done." He laughed a little and I relaxed a lot. "Oh sweetheart. You're open for me." He sounded like it was a miracle and began moving out, then went back in.

"Don't stop." I begged despite the pinching pain of my innocence being forever lost to the man I love. "I want to feel you. All of you."

"Baseball, football, soccer."

I giggled, "What are you doing?"

"Trying not to lose it already."

"So I suppose it wouldn't help if I said things like, lace, thigh-high leather boots, cleavage . . .

He picked up speed causing me to take a sharp breath as the sensations overwhelmed me. "Barbara!!"

"Don't stop!!" I cried out as I lost all control of my body and clenched around him in one gloriously fulfilling release.

"Oh shit!!" He cried out and arched his own back like a cobra as he spent his seed deep inside me.

I ran my hands up his chest and over his shoulders. "You are so beautiful."

He smiled and looked down for me, "I don't think men are supposed to be beautiful. handsome, sexy maybe, but not beautiful. You're beautiful."

"I'll try to come up with a better word later. Right now I want to do that again."

"Again? Already?"

I nodded with what I'm sure is a goofy smile.

He tried to look scoldingly at me, but I can see he's much too happy to be taken seriously. "In a few minutes. I take it you're not going shoe shopping?"

"Are you going to make love to me again?"

He rolled and sat me on top of him without ever leaving me. I'm sure he's plenty ready now, but wants me to rest for a minute before we begin again. "As often as I can for the rest of our lives."

For the second time in the last few weeks, I took another first ride.

Epilogue

Lou and I were married two months later. Our honeymoon lasted a month inside his house. We had plenty to keep us busy with unpacking and rearranging of our new furnishings. He'd insisted we not travel because of the virus. Having traveled enough in my lifetime I was happy to just have him to myself while we played house and started our new life together.

Paulie is still and issue, and dismantling the businesses is still a constant battle, but with Myles and Lou at my side things are manageable. I went ahead and had the outpatient surgery that put a clamp on my tubes. Lou agreed we could adopt if we ever really wanted kids. I'm thinking that will work itself out in due time. Right now I'm very happy to have Lou to myself.

Once I was healthy enough, I started spending more time with Liz and a few other girls I'd bonded with in the kitchen that day. A day that seems so far away. Almost as far away as my old life. I don't even feel like the old

Barbara Whitmore anymore. I am Barbara Colson to my husband, and Bobby to my friends.

My friends. That's new too. Red, Salina, who I text several times a day and talk to at least once a week. Liz and I are talking about starting a catering business. Lou is hesitant of course, but he doesn't argue with me too much anymore. He's still on eggshells over my health and we are still discussing the architectural company.

I received a letter from Paulie Macaroni, that's all he is to me, earlier today. Part of me wanted to rip it up and throw it away without reading it. The other part knew better.

I opened the envelope and unfolded the single sheet of paper.

Dearest Daughter,

> *Your recent health problems do not change anything. However, I see you're dissolving Mr. Whitmore's assets as quickly as possible. This does change things.*
>
> *As you know you can't squeeze blood from a turnip, and I have been advised not to engage in a war with your husband's family. Therefore your life and well being will not come into jeopardy via myself.*
>
> *This is not to say you are safe shall we happen to cross paths in the future. I*

*suggest you see we do not. I will say one
thing daughter, well-played.*

Your Father—Paulie

Lou snatched the letter from my hands, "What's this?"

"A letter from Paulie. I didn't know you were home."

"I see that. I've been standing here for two minutes while you read this. How was it delivered?"

"The mail I guess. Don't get worked up, he's not going to bother me anymore."

"He didn't exactly say you were safe either." He argued folding the letter and shoving it in his inside cut pocket.

"At least I know he won't cause you and the club problems."

"Men like that lie, Barbara. I'm going to put a couple prospects on you for a while just in case."

"Like I'm not surrounded by enough bikers??" I teased.

He wrapped his arms around me and kissed my neck, "Just think, you've only met three chapters and a couple HOGs."

I went from having no family, to one so large I don't think I'll ever meet them all, but I love them all anyway. Just like they loved me enough to put me in the center of a loving motorcycle parade on our wedding day. Talk about a big biker hug!